More praise for
The Autobiography of Foudini M. Cat

"If you are enchanted by slowly twitching tails, unblinking eyes, and the unique brand of arrogant independence that only a house cat can exude, read on."

—*Rocky Mountain News*

"At times cautionary, occasionally whimsical, his story will amuse the cat lover immensely and provide pearls of wisdom for the kittens of the world."

—*Weekly Alibi*

"Bittersweet . . . Schaeffer is not the first serious writer to go cooing after her kitties; T. S. Eliot comes to mind, as does May Sarton. Yet Foudini soon emerges an interesting creature in his own right."

—*Washington City Paper*

"Schaeffer has done an excellent job of capturing the essence of felinity: if cats could talk, they'd sound like Foudini. . . . Schaeffer has made Foudini so believable that your friendly reviewer actually found himself idly wondering for a brief moment: 'I wonder what Foudini will think of this review?' "

—*Authors Review of Books* (on-line)

"[A] wonderful story . . . Endowed with much love, wisdom, and joy . . . This is one of those delightful little books that one treasures, one gives to loved ones, and one reads to children and friends . . . Warm, witty and endearing."

—*The Ellenville Press*

"Whimsical . . . Magnificent fiction . . . Every page is pure enjoyment. . . . Schaeffer captures the wonder, intelligence, and dignity of cats."

—*Utica, Shelby Source* (MI)

"Touching . . . Foudini narrates his own tale matter-of-factly and with nice catty irony. This cat is no fool, and he offers an unsentimental perspective on the people with whom he lives."

—*Library Journal*

ALSO BY SUSAN FROMBERG SCHAEFFER

THE AUTOBIOGRAPHY OF FOUDINI M. CAT

THE
AUTOBIOGRAPHY OF
FOUDINI M. CAT

SUSAN FROMBERG SCHAEFFER

FAWCETT BOOKS

NEW YORK

A Fawcett Book
Published by The Ballantine Publishing Group

http://www.randomhouse.com/BB/

Library of Congress Catalog Card Number: 98-96310

ISBN 0-449-91145-4

Cover design by Barbara Leff
Cover photo by Bruno Blumenfeld

This edition published by arrangement with Alfred A. Knopf,
a division of Random House, Inc.

Manufactured in the United States of America

First Ballantine Books Edition: November 1998

10 9 8 7 6 5 4 3 2 1

For Neil

THE

AUTOBIOGRAPHY

OF

FOUDINI

M.

CAT

HOUSECAT

BY

HIMSELF

AUTHOR'S PREFACE

I CAME INTO THE WORLD like everything else that is
born, willy-nilly, but books are not born in this way.
There is always a reason for the existence of a book, and
let us hope it is a good one. The occasion for writing this
book was the arrival of Grace the Cat, a small and very
young gray country cat from Mouse House, who is sleek
and shiny and altogether beautiful, and who has enormous tufts of gray fur growing out of her ears. Grace the
Cat has been assigned to me by the woman, and so she is
my responsibility.

She is, in many ways, a most interesting cat, although
she is not at all like me, as she is forever bent on mischief.
But because I am an older and wiser cat, Grace the Cat
looks to me for counsel and an explanation of the world

and the way it works, and so I have allowed Grace the Cat (henceforward usually referred to as "Grace") to prevail upon me to set down the story of my life as a housecat in the human world.

There will be many lessons Grace can learn from my story, although she does not seem in a hurry to learn lessons, because at this very moment, she is leaping at the hand of my Assigned Person, who has foolishly let herself linger on the landing, her hand on the banister. A human hand with five fingers dangling downward, moving ever so slightly, is inevitably an irresistible temptation to such a young cat as Grace, who is, you might say, demented with youth.

Grace the Cat is not like me, but already I have come to love her. The story of my life from now on will be, to a great extent, the story of her life, and since she is such a precipitous and foolish cat, it cannot hurt her to know what to expect from existence so that she can begin to resign herself and to adjust, as all housecats must.

I say all this because I want you to understand that it is not simple vanity that leads me to write my autobiography. I am not a very vain cat. Cats have quite an undeserved reputation for vanity and aloofness and independence, when what we ought to be celebrated for is our ability to exist alone and to dream. If other cats are like me—and I am not sure they are, but I think they must be—I would say that cats in general are contemplative animals who are easily satisfied and perhaps overly pre-occupied by their own thoughts. That may be our worst sin: how content and pleased we are with our meditations upon the world around us—once we have left our kittenhood behind us, that is.

I cannot say that Grace is terribly pensive, although she is still a kitten. She is only one year old, and may change, although I doubt it. Even as I write, Grace is jumping up onto a chair and banging her head into the slats of its back. For some time, I thought she was an extremely clumsy cat, but now I realize that the trouble is in her eyes. She only sees clearly when something is far away, and so she often jumps up onto low tables or kitchen counters or tops of headboards and finds herself dangling by her claws. She has just leaped onto a banister landing and fallen down to the floor below. Grace is no judge of distance. It is because she has so little judgment that I am writing this book. I wonder what she will make of it.

Having exhausted herself rolling about in catnip, Grace has now curled up on the rug and wrapped her extravagantly longhaired and fluffy tail about her, and so I will begin.

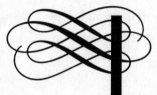

In the beginning, I was not a housecat.

I was born in a wall. And when I was born, it was very cold. Water had frozen everywhere, so it was difficult to find water to drink, and snow fell constantly, so my mother would spend a great deal of her time searching for food and for a warm place for the two of us to live. I do not myself remember the long, exhausting searches for food, the nervous prowlings on streets waiting for an opportunity to slit open a plastic trash bag, although my mother told me of this, but I do remember the terrible cold. I remember shivering until I was exhausted, and I remember how thin my mother grew, until her ribs protruded through her fur, and she was not as soft to sleep upon as she had been when I first came to myself in the world.

My mother was an intelligent and farsighted cat, because she did eventually find us an exceptionally good home. She came upon an apartment building whose basement window was loose. She dragged me through the space between window and wall, and we found ourselves in a warm basement, which became even warmer and more lovely whenever the washing machines and dryers were in use. My mother found out the warmest and safest places, and taught me to sleep in them. I slept beneath a dryer and behind a washing machine, and my mother saw to it that I hid when anyone came down to use the machines.

This was a good place for a cat to live in the middle of the winter. There were many mice when we first came, and my mother caught them, and we ate them, but soon she had caught all the mice there were. We ran out of food, and after three days with nothing to eat, my mother went back out through the window to hunt for something to eat. Of course I expected to see her again. I expected to hear her voice, saying, *Look what I have for you.* I didn't realize that she would never come back. Who would have thought such a thing was possible? But she never returned, and I was left to fend for myself in the basement, where I was warm, if hungry. One day, a mouse ran right in front of me, and I tried to leap upon it, but it was faster than I was, and ran away. It takes a long time to become a good mouser, and many small cats die of hunger before they learn to hunt. It is not an easy world.

Do you hear that, Grace, sleeping on your warm rug in front of the hot-air vent? It is not an easy world. Don't make that mistake. I remember having heard of a house-cat who was taken to the country and was for the first time let out-of-doors. Without looking either to the right or to the left, he walked straight into the woods, and if his person hadn't rushed after him and swept him up, he would have been eaten by raccoons. But how could he know better, when for years the entire household had revolved around him?

One day I came out from behind the dryer, intending once again to look for a mouse, but my four legs were weak beneath me, and I sat down in the middle of the cold cement floor. Just then a man and a woman walked in, and the woman said, "Oh, look, a tiny cat!" She came over to me and tried to pick me up, but I had seen how my mother defended herself against these human creatures, and I was a sensible cat, if tiny, so I hissed at her, rolled over on my back, and extended my still-thin claws. Then I fled back to my residence behind the dryer.

"That cat is wild," the man said.

"That cat is starving," the woman said. "I wonder what happened to his mother?" Then they said how wise my mother had been to hide me in a warm basement, and I was pleased to hear this, because, young as I was, I knew it was true.

Later, as I grew ever more hungry, I began to come out

into the open more and more, and it seemed that whenever I appeared, so did the woman, who each time tried to catch me, but I was too fast for her. When she saw her attempts were useless, she brought down a plate of dry food. The smell was delicious, but the small, hard pieces were too difficult to chew. When the woman saw this, she poured a glass of warm milk into the dish, and this softened the food enough so that I began to eat. The woman seemed very pleased, and I grew to like her, but I never ate without watching her carefully out of the corner of my eye, lest she once again lunge and try to capture me. But she would only watch me and smile.

And then one day she came down with a cardboard box, and I knew immediately that she planned on packing me into it, and so I began to hide from her again. Now she waited longer to feed me, waited until she was sure I would be truly hungry, so that I would once more eat from the dish while she watched me. Still, as soon as she reached out to touch me, I was back behind the dryer. I was a clever cat, like my mother, and had no intention of letting myself be caught and winding up in someone's stew pot, which is what my mother said happened to foolish kittens who let anyone and everyone who walked by scratch them behind their ears.

I would have been safe from that woman, and my life would have been entirely different, if I had not come down with a cold. Immediately after I began sneezing, my eyes grew crusty and runny. When the woman saw this, she redoubled her efforts to catch me.

As it turned out, all she had to do was wait. My eyes itched and oozed, and sometimes when I blinked, my eyelids stuck together and I had to blink hard to get my eyes open. And then one day my eyelids stuck together, and nothing I could do would make them open. I rubbed them with my paw. I licked my paws and rubbed again, but my eyes were stuck, and firmly stuck. I could see nothing at all. When I smelled the plate of food, I staggered blindly out from behind the dryer, and suddenly I heard a loud noise. The woman had dropped her carton over me, and I was in her cardboard box at last. Today is the day I will be eaten, I said to myself. She has been fattening me up.

But the woman did not eat me. She took me to a building where someone put drops in my eyes so that they opened, although they were still crusty. There were men in white suits called doctors and many cats and dogs in cages. I was put in one of these cages and quickly went to sleep because I was tired and had no hope of getting out. Every few hours, a hand reached in for me, and I was stuck with a sharp needle, and a glass tube was inserted in the opening beneath my tail. I was terrified, and again and again I thought, These people mean to kill me. Whenever I heard anyone come near my cage, I began to hiss and spit and claw until finally they wrapped me in a towel to keep themselves safe from me. At last I began to feel stronger.

"He is wild and insane and vicious," the doctor told the woman who had brought me there. The woman said that even so she would have liked to take me home, but my very presence made her sneeze. "How odd that is, when I love cats better than anything else," she said.

Are you listening, Grace? It is a terrible world, when our mere presence makes some people sneeze and cough and choke and break out in red welts. Not everyone will be happy to see you! Not everyone will fight over you! Not everyone wants you sitting in his lap!

She is paying no attention. I can tell.

The doctor said that if no one came for me, he would have to put me to sleep. I thought how unnecessary that was, since I put myself to sleep countless times a day, but of course now I understand that he meant something altogether different.

Finally, a man and a woman came to the building, which I learned was an animal hospital. The woman's cat had just died, and she asked the doctor if he happened to have another she might look at. They grabbed me up by the fur at the back of my neck and brought me out, hissing and spitting as usual, but this woman ignored my behavior and picked me up and placed me inside her warm and furry coat. I was so surprised I didn't struggle. And for no reason I can explain, I felt quite happy there, snuggled against her, and I went to sleep. She petted me with only one finger, and this was pleasant, since I was still very small.

"Do you want him?" the doctor asked her, and she said she would have to think about it. She came back the next day and said she would take me as long as I was healthy.

"Oh, he is very healthy," the doctor said, and when I was once again snuggled up against the woman inside her coat, and when she was ready to leave with me, he handed her a bag with a bottle of medicine for my pneumonia and a tube of salve for my eyes. If I had not already been safe and snug inside her coat, she said, she would have left me there, because I was not, as anyone could see, a healthy cat.

So I am to be eaten at last, I thought. Because this is what most cats expect of people. They expect people to trap them and eat them. It is one of the many memories of our previous lives passed on to us at birth, and those of us who have lived outside even for a short time, living by our wits, hunting mice and slow birds, have these memories. We have dreams in which humans come upon us, their eyes full of knives and forks and plates. And because this is what I believed, I was determined to keep myself out of this new woman's hands.

They took me to their house, and I was locked in a soft

room. It had a thick carpet on the floor, and in a corner there was a small couch beneath which I could hide. But I found that if the woman lay down on the floor and reached out for me when I was under the couch, she could seize me, and so I hid in the dark beneath a bookcase and refused to come out. The woman's arm would not fit beneath the bookcase, and I thought I had found an excellent hiding place.

But she was determined to get hold of me. Human beings must be excellent mousers; they have such patience. Day after day, she lay on the floor, poking at me with a long stick until I would move closer to her, and then she would hold on to me and pet me. I was growing accustomed to this strange petting until one day she seized me and poured white powder all over me. A few days later, she fastened a lavender collar around my neck. After this, I was frightened and insulted and decided I would never come out again, but I grew hungry, and after some time I grew to like the pettings, which made me warm and sleepy and reminded me of my mother, licking me with her sandy tongue from head to tail. And so gradually we grew to be friends. At least I did not hide when she came into the room, and after a while, I would lie out in the open, on a chair, and watch her. You grow tired of being frightened, and one day I thought, If I am going to be eaten, then let her eat me. I am tired of frightening myself silly.

There comes a time when you resign yourself to your fate, whatever it may be. I have not yet reached such a time, but I have seen someone else who has.

Of course, Grace believes it is no trouble at all to resign herself to her fate, but that is because her fate has, so far, been so pleasant.

Just as I was beginning to like this tall woman, who at first resembled a tree to my eyes, she came for me in the room in which she kept me and picked me up and put me in a blue box, and as I heard her closing the box, I scolded myself. I asked myself, Why didn't you struggle? How could you be so foolish as to trust her? Now you will certainly be eaten.

But it was even worse than I thought. The woman took me in my box out to the car and brought me back to the hospital. She didn't want me after all. She was going to leave me there. When the same doctor who had stabbed me before picked me up again and once more stuck me with something sharp, and once again thrust a glass tube beneath my tail, my despair can barely be imagined. But then the most amazing thing happened! He let go of me! And I saw the open blue box, and I could smell it, and it smelled, not of the hospital, but of the woman's home, and obeying an impulse that even today seems strange, I jumped away from the doctor and back into the blue box, and once in, I sat up and I stared reproachfully at the woman.

"Look at that!" the doctor said. "That crazy, vicious cat!"

"Can I take him home now?" the woman asked.

And she took me home, back to the red room with the soft rug and the soft chairs and the metal square in the floor through which warm air blew. I soon took to sleeping on that metal square until I heard approaching footsteps. Then, to be safe, I retreated beneath the bookcase. By now I came out when I heard the woman's voice and smelled the warm food she brought me on a nice warm plate.

I remembered an old cat who lived with us in my wall telling me that human beings on the street were not to be trusted, but every once in a while, one of them came along who loved and understood cats, and then the extremely fortunate cat—usually a kitten, he said sadly, almost always a kitten—was taken to a warm place where lights shone both day and night and where it was never, ever cold, and where the people existed only to feed and pet that cat, and those cats didn't sleep on the floor at night. No, they slept in soft beds upon pillows stuffed with birds' feathers, and they grew fat and happy and spent their days dreaming dreams from the beginning of the history of cats, and so in the end, they became the Learned Cats, the Wise Ones. What an enviable destiny that is, he said.

His bones poked through his fur, as my mother's did,

and his teeth were brown and loose, and so he had trouble chewing his mice when he caught them, and as a consequence was reduced to slitting open garbage bags, as my mother was also doing, a shameful activity for a cat, he said, but one to which old age had driven him. But while he lived with us, my mother would chew his mouse for him, and then leave it between his paws, and he would gnaw slowly on it. In return, he would bring my mother partially gnawed chicken bones and bits of fish still attached to their skeletons.

I think of him often these days, and wonder if he was my father.

After several days back in the warm red room, I began to forgive the woman and spent less and less time under the bookcase and more and more time in the pools of light that formed on the nice warm scratchy rug that had the delightful texture of my mother's tongue. That is where I was, peacefully sleeping, when the woman came in, seized me, and once more thrust me into the blue box with the grating on one side. I was so unhappy I began to wail, and when the woman talked to me in a soft voice, I became angry and lay down in the box and turned my back to the grating, against which the woman had now pressed her face.

My worst suspicions were now immediately confirmed. The woman picked me up in my box and carried me out to the car. Where could we be going, but to the doctor's? But it was worse than I had imagined! Just as I was preparing myself for the slam of the door, an enormous panting and whining animal jumped into the car and stood over my box. A dog!

Inside my box, I could feel his hot breath. It was like a wind. He pressed his large, wet black nose to my box and cried with eagerness to eat me. I gathered up my courage and turned myself to the grating and then, when he had once more pressed his nose against the grating, and when I could see his enormous brown eyes, I dashed forward and smacked him through the wire grating. I smacked him hard with my nails out. And what a howling he set up! The woman turned around and began stroking the monster dog's head, and finally he lay down on the floor next to my box, gazing sorrowfully at me, and every now and then whimpering, with disappointment, no doubt, since he must have realized that eating me was going to be no easy matter.

And through all this, the woman kept saying, *Nice cat, good cat, what a beautiful cat, you are my cat, what a nice cat you are, don't worry about him, he's not going to bother you.*

Not going to bother me! When through my grating swept gusts of his warm, hot breath, like the breath over those gratings in the street where my mother and I used to sleep on the coldest nights.

Oh, I said to myself, is this what life will be like? A few

happy hours in a soft room with a soft floor, and then yanked away without warning, put in a box with a grating, and taken God knows where? And I heard my mother's sorrowful voice saying, Kitten, life is hard and full of disappointments, but if you are careful, it can be a good life, and we are so made that we forget the bad things that have happened to us, and when we find a warm piece of meat or a patch of catnip, we believe that the world has always been wonderful. But we must be careful always because the world is full of creatures who want to eat us or worse, and the worst of these creatures is the dog.

I said, "Tell me about dogs," and my mother said, "You hear that loud voice barking? That is the voice of a dog. Some dogs are so big that you can run between their legs and never brush against their stomachs. And they have big teeth! Very big teeth! Stay away from dogs!"

"Will they eat me up?" I asked her.

"If they can," she said.

But she would tell me no more about dogs. "You are a small cat," she said, "and all small cats dream about dogs. Your dreams will tell you all you need to know." But I had not yet had these dreams. I thought, I will have to use my own judgment about this dog.

And just then the dog wriggled closer to my box and recklessly pressed his nose into the grating. Quick as a flash I again hit him on the nose. The dog wailed in outrage. "Oh, no," said the woman, who was in the front seat. She turned around, picked me up in my blue box, and set me on her lap and began talking to me—*What a good cat you are, don't worry about that dog, that dog never hurt anything in his life, that dog likes cats*—and other such nonsense.

There are human beings, my mother had said, who will do anything to get you into their stew pot. You must watch carefully. Sometimes a human friend is only a patient woman with an excellent recipe for fried cat.

Fried cat!

At least I was now far from the dog. Perhaps she intended to feed me to the dog.

We had been in the car for some time now, and still we had not come to the hospital. Had the stupid person driving the car lost his way? Would we never get there? I grew quite sleepy, and as soon as my eyes closed entirely, I began to dream I was an enormous cat lying along a thick bough of a tree, and beneath me gray wolves with red eyes were leaping up against the tree trunk, their eyes on me, their jaws covered with foam. Dogs!

My eyes snapped open. Didn't the dog in the car look exactly like those wolves? He did! He was not even a dog. He was a wolf!

Nice cat, good cat, the woman said. But I could see through her. She was a keeper of wolves. I was in a car with a wolf! As soon as the car stopped, I decided, I would make my escape.

But when the car finally stopped, the woman carried me out in my box, and I was taken into a house I'd never seen before. This house was full of wonderful smells, smells I recognized immediately. They were mouse smells, wonderful and fragrant, which made my tail twitch this way and that, and there were smells of other animals, larger and more dangerous. *Woodchucks, raccoons,* a voice whispered between my ears, and I realized it was my dream voice talking to me.

This is a mousey house, I thought as the woman carried my cage through the rooms. I like this house better than the city house. I will escape soon and hunt for mice.

But the woman knew my intentions. She took me to a small blue room and set my box on the floor. I saw the door to the room and thought, As soon as she opens my box, I will escape through that door.

The woman pulled the door until it clicked shut, and then she opened my box. I looked around carefully before I was ready to climb out. The woman watched me. Then I saw the chest of drawers and scurried over to it and squeezed myself beneath it.

"Not again," said the woman.

She went out, closed the door behind her, and when she came back, she had a dish of food with her. It was warm and steamy and delicious, and I was hungry because it had been a long drive to this mousey house, but I stayed in my hiding place. When she goes away, I thought, I will come out to eat. She will never find the excellent new hiding place I've discovered this time.

While she was gone, I had investigated the room and discovered that the bottom drawer of the bureau was open. I climbed in and saw that there was a dark place behind the drawer. How could anyone reach me in there? How could anyone guess where I was? I jumped into the dark place behind the drawer. I tucked my paws beneath me and congratulated myself on having found such a perfect place so quickly.

But when the woman came with my plate, she refused to leave the room. She sat on the bed next to my plate of food, and she began to call me—*Foudini! Foudini!*

I would ignore her, I thought, and then she would go away, and I could creep from my very dark place behind the bottom drawer.

But she was not going to go away, and every instant I grew hungrier, until finally I said a quick goodbye to this world and climbed over the back panel of the drawer and fell into the drawer itself, *thump, thump,* and then climbed over the front of the drawer and jumped down onto the carpet. Another carpet, smelling this time of mice! Recent mice, fresh mice, live mice!

I went over to the bed. It was high off the ground. I climbed up the bedspread, and when I got to the top, there was a dish of the most delicious food, so naturally I threw caution to the winds and began eating, and while I ate, the woman stroked my head and back.

I will not be taken in by you another time! I swore to myself as I chewed, and just then I heard the dog bark, the worst sound I'd ever heard, a noise so loud it made the walls shake, and I thought, It is true what the old cat said. Cats are not conceited animals. They are quiet, and quietly go about, mindful of others, careful to cause no trouble. Dogs are the arrogant ones. A dog announces what it has to say at the top of its lungs, convinced the entire world is interested and ought to be listening. Does a cat do this? No! Except under the most extraordinary circumstances. Beware of the world when you hear a cat scream! But a dog will shout everything down. He will drown out every voice and every noise and never think twice. A postman on the street will set off a riot of dog voices. A cat will see the postman coming and will only watch quietly from beneath a bush. Dogs, the old cat said, annoy the entire world.

So I finished my meal and retreated to my place behind the drawer. But this time it was harder to get behind the drawer because I had eaten so much that my sides were puffed out, and when I tried to slide over the back wall of the drawer, I had to try twice, and a disagreeable sensation it was, the feel of the wood pushing into my extremely round stomach.

Next time eat less, I told myself, but the next time, I immediately ate everything on the plate, and it seemed to me that my stomach grew even rounder.

"I'm afraid to feed him any more," the woman said. "He looks as if he's swallowed a shoe box. He might explode."

"He'll eat as much as you give him," the man said. "After all, he was once a starving cat."

And so for many days I lived behind my drawer in the blue room, coming out only when the woman came in with my dish of food, my ears always tilted toward the door, listening for the dog, who was often on the other side, whimpering, and I thought, Well you may whimper, you monstrosity. You are not coming in here. You are not eating me, and if you try, I will get you on the nose.

Then I would remember how big he was, and I would go behind my drawer and cry. When he heard me cry, he would scratch at the door, as if, in his eagerness to eat me, he had quite forgotten how the woman would shout at him when she saw his claw marks on the wood.

I thought, This is not a bad life, really. The room is warm and the rug is deep and during the day warm sun falls on the carpet, and there are two flies to chase who buzz about most interestingly, and several spiders whom I leap at, trying to catch them in my paws, and there is a window I can sit at, and I can look down the meadow, and there is the wonderful smell of mice coming closer, and even a marvelous scratching in the walls, and one day soon a mouse will run out and I will be after him and I will get him, just as my mother used to do.

But I should have known! Grace, I should have known! Pay attention to this, Grace! Whenever the room is delightfully warm, whenever we have been well fed, whenever we think ourselves safe from harm, whenever we are foolish enough to congratulate ourselves on our happy fates, *then* we are in for trouble! Trouble with a tail, Grace! Trouble with a drill or a broom or a mop, Grace! Battle stations, Grace! Hiding places! We must always be ready to run for our lives! Always!

Is Grace listening? She is not listening. She is awake now, throwing her toy mouse up in the air and chasing it across the room. Soon she will be lying on her back, her lovely gray stomach exposed to the air, wiggling this way and that, showing the world how attractive she is. The woman will come in and say, *What a lovely cat, what an attractive cat, so gray, so smooth, so shiny!* And Grace will grow mad with happiness. When there could be an alligator walking in from the kitchen! When a dog might have climbed in through an open window! When anything might happen! But what does Grace expect to happen? She expects that one day a bird will obligingly fly straight into her mouth. She sits on the shelf near the kitchen window, and when she sees birds at the feeder, she talks to them, asking them to come in. *Come closer,* she says. She makes up names for the birds. She calls them Flying Feathered Feasts. She likes to watch them when it rains, because then they are Flying Feathered Feasts with Gravy.

All cats are poets in their hearts. All cats like to make up strange names for things. Grace the Cat is not alone in this. I myself made up several poems and songs when I was a young cat, and now I repeat them to myself whenever the house is empty or sad. It is wise to do certain things when you are young so you will have them to think about when you are older.

Grace is again crying to the birds. "Foolish animal!" I tell her. "You will scare them away." But she looks at me with wide, blank eyes and goes on attempting to persuade the birds into her mouth. She is a terrible exasperation to me at times, and a wonder. Such an optimistic animal! So optimistic she does not deserve the name "cat." But then her early life was not like mine. Still, no matter *what* my early life had been, I would have grown into a cautious cat. Even when I was quite a small cat, the woman would pick me up and say, "This cat has heavy bones." They were heavy, with caution and worry, and not only my own worries—oh, no. I had the dog's worries as well. But I am getting ahead of myself.

I think I will get up, casually, as if only to stroll about the room, and then I will leap upon Grace the Cat and chase her into the basement and up into the rafters. Not because I am angry at her, although there is almost always a good reason to be angry at such a senseless creature, but because I want her to remember that at any moment something large may leap upon you, and it is important to know how to reach the rafters as quickly as possible. Once you are safely in the rafters, someone would have to tear the house down to get his hands on you.

"Who is trying to get his hands on me, and what is bad about that?" asks Grace the Most Petted. Imprudent only-one-year-old thing! She has never had to face down a dog in order to reach her bowl of food! If she knew! If she knew what my life had been like!

Dogs? Grace the Cat asks me. Are they nice?

After all I have told her!

You see how difficult it is to pass on knowledge? To pass on even one single thing? But I never give up. *Some* grain of understanding may yet flower in Grace's hopelessly happy little brain. And so I will go on with my story.

After I had grown quite accustomed to my nice blue room, its two flies and its spiders, its delicious and promising aroma of mice, the door periodically opening to admit the woman and her splendid plates of food, after I was quite resigned to living in that room forever, knowing that I was safe from the dog who lived on the other side of the door, the woman came and left the door open.

And right behind her was the dog!

You must not think I exaggerate when I say this was no ordinary dog. He looked like a wolf, but he was larger than a wolf. I know that I am short, and at that time, I was even shorter and smaller, but when this dog stretched out on the floor of my blue room, which he promptly did, he was as long as the bed! If you counted his tail, that is—and I did—because when his tail hit the door or the chest of drawers, it made a terrible *thwack.*

You must look out for that tail, I told myself. And those teeth! I had never seen such large teeth. And his mouth! Big enough to swallow me down whole as if I were a smooth round bit of dry food.

I will not be eaten so fast, I told myself in my hiding place behind the bottom drawer of this new, mousey house, and even though I was shivering with fear and my heart was thumping hard, I began to make my plans.

The dog, meanwhile, crept up to the chest of drawers and whined—such piteous sounds, if he had not been a dog, I would have felt sorry for him. But he did not paw at the chest of drawers. He did not growl. He seemed to wait for me as I lurked in front of a baseboard behind the bed, that baseboard where the essence of mouse was particularly strong.

Finally he got tired of me, and he went out.

So, I thought, all I have to do is wait patiently, and the dog will go about his business, because dogs, as everyone knows, have no patience whatever, and then I can come out, climb on the bed, and eat my dinner.

But there was no dinner!

From the kitchen came the delightful smells of my dinner, cooking. And I was hungry. I expected the woman to come in and call me and put my dinner up on the bed. When she didn't come, I was dizzy with hunger and disbelief, and I wanted to go into the kitchen and howl my head off until the woman produced my plate.

She had forgotten me! But the dog hadn't.

Every so often, he came into the room and lay down in front of the chest of drawers, and when he did, I raised up my head and hissed as loudly and fiercely as possible. Then I went to sleep, because what else could I do?

Finally, I was too hungry to stay hidden behind the drawer, and so I climbed out and scurried beneath one piece of furniture to another until I came to the kitchen. And what did I see? The woman was carrying a plate across the room—fried liver and bread. Of course it was for me!

But she didn't give it to me. She set the plate down in front of the woodstove, and the dog, *the dog,* went up to the plate as if he were entitled to every morsel. This was too much for me, and I forgot all my mother's good advice. I forgot my dream about wolves standing up against the big tree, pawing its bark, whining in their eagerness to reach a cat who lay along the tree bough. I forgot all this, and I flew beneath the woodstove, and as soon as the dog moved forward to begin eating, I sprang forward and whacked him across the nose!

The dog let out a shriek.

I grabbed a piece of liver, retreated back under the stove, and ate it.

The dog was still whining, and I was still hungry, so I leaped forward again, stole another piece of liver, and retreated once more to a safe distance. The huge dog rubbed at his huge nose with his enormous paw, and while he did this, I flew forward and bit into another piece of liver. Now the dog made a kind of pleading noise, and as I chewed, hastily, fearing the dog would soon sweep up everything on his plate with one swipe of his immense tongue, I noticed that the dog seemed little inclined to hurt me. He was not pressing his head beneath the woodstove to bring his great jaw and teeth closer to me, as he could easily have done. He was not growling. No, he lay in front of his plate, whining quietly, staring at me with mournful eyes.

"That is a ferocious cat," the woman said. "The dog will never get anything to eat."

I ate pieces of liver until my stomach was quite bulgy, and then I lay down, pressing myself up against the wall in back of the stove.

Finally, the dog dared to approach his plate, and as I had foreseen, he cleaned the dish with one swipe of his great tongue.

I suppose now he will try to eat me, I thought, but the dog had lost all interest in me and was standing next to the woman's chair, complaining about the loss of his delicious pieces of liver, while she stroked his big ears. Eventually, the dog lay down and went to sleep, and I scurried back to my blue room and my hiding place behind the drawer. Once I was there, I felt perfectly safe, safe and well stuffed.

How little we know, Grace, of what the future holds in store for us! Which is why we must do more than dance and leap about and sharpen our claws on thready furniture and dangle from curtains just beneath the ceiling when we have climbed them! Which is why we must study what is going on around us, not merely annoy ourselves and everyone else as we try to move into the attractive rooms of a dolls' house, which is what you did only last week. Everyone standing about, looking at the dolls' house, saying, It looks as if a cat got at it, and then your gray paw came curling out of the dining room window.

Oh, how little self-control you have! And hadn't I told you the rooms were too small for us? Hadn't I told you I'd done the same thing years before, when I myself was a small cat? Didn't I say, The rooms look large, but they are not. It is a mistake of our eyes. And did you listen?

Certainly not. And yet you were more fortunate than I was. Your collar did not get caught by a hook on the dolls'-house wall. You did not have to endure a storm of reproaches until you were freed.

I have consulted with myself and asked myself if it is wise to tell Grace what happened next, and how surprising was my life after I began to leave my blue room and impudently walk past the dog. As you now know, Grace is not a wise cat. She is a happy cat, and probably for that very reason she is not very cautious. She sits in bathtubs, beneath the tub faucet, and lets the water drip onto her head while she decides whether to swat at the drops. She doesn't know whether she is a cat or a fish, and she refuses to discuss what is appropriate and advisable for a young cat. Is it judicious of me to tell a remarkable story to such a flighty-minded cat? This story should tell the reader how unpredictable life can be. From this story, one should learn that the worst does not always happen and that it is quite as bad to be too doomful as it is to be too sanguine. Ah, well. We will see if she learns anything. I can only try.

Day followed day in Mouse House, as I had come to call it, and now when I left my room and took up my position beneath the woodstove, the dog barely took notice of me.

He is only waiting until I become too confident, and then he will swallow me, I thought.

But he didn't seem interested in swallowing me.

He appeared to be interested in the smallest thing I did. If I went into the living room and chased a spool of thread, he would lie near the entrance to the room and watch me. If I saw a fly and leaped up into the air, clapping my paws together in order to catch and eat it, he observed me with unending curiosity. Every now and then he would try to speak to me, not barking, but imitating, I saw, my own voice. And after a while, I began to think, Perhaps he is not really a dog or a wolf after all.

He is a dog, said the voices of my ancestors. *Keep clear of him.*

And then one day I batted a ball of crumpled aluminum foil across the room, and it came to rest between the dog's front paws. The dog looked down at the ball, and then looked at me with expectant interest. What would I do now?

And I would never have predicted it, I would never have thought myself capable of such a rash act, but I danced across the room, my back arched, my fur standing on end, and ran right beneath the dog's huge jaws and batted the ball away from him.

The dog observed me with attention, his big ears up, his tail beginning to wag.

I hit the ball so that it flew right past him. But he didn't chase it. He watched it, and then he looked at me again. What did I want him to do?

He continued to watch me, so eagerly, so expectantly, that I was utterly transported, far beyond common sense, far beyond the voices of my mother and my ancestors, and I hurtled across the room as fast as I could go and ran up the dog's enormous nose and ran between his ears and let myself slide down his shiny side.

The dog stood up and looked down at me, and I prepared to hit him once again on the nose, but he only made a questioning noise, something halfway between a purr and a growl, and he lay down again. So I did it once more. I flew across the room, up the dog's nose, across the great plain between his ears, and this time I lay there, my back legs dangling down over his eyes and his mouth.

This was not as foolhardy as it may seem, because if the dog had growled or tried to bite me, I could easily have raked him with my back paws.

The dog made a contented little sound and went on lying on the rug, in the sun, a cat on his head, a cat's leg dangling down on either side of his nose.

From that day on, we became friends. We ate from the same dish.

This pleased the woman, who said, "Look at that!"

"Look at that," the man said, when I lay on the floor next to the dog, and the dog got up, sniffed me, and washed me down with one lick of his tongue. I wasn't sure I liked these washings. When my mother had washed me, she washed me slowly, one small piece at a time, and her sandy tongue made its way down through my fur to my skin, and when she was finished, I was shiny and clean. But after the dog washed me, my fur was wet and I was cold and my fur was sticky and stood straight up in the air. I had to clean myself all over again.

Naturally, I believed that the dog wanted me to wash him in return. After all, there were places he could not reach, not even with his enormous tongue. I set about cleaning him behind his ears and, when he lay stretched out on the rug, beneath his chin. But he did not appreciate my efforts. He would yelp and shriek when I finally reached down to the skin beneath his fur, and then I would lose my temper and put out my nails and attempt to hold him in place while I finished. When I did this, he would get up, and I would slide down his side onto the floor. Then I would hide beneath a sofa until he walked by, and I would jump out at him or dance sideways at him, my fur standing on end, or I would follow him and jump up and grab his tail. After I had made many successful attacks on his tail, I would forgive him for his ungrateful shrieking and yelping, and then I would run at him and annoy him until he got up and began to chase me. In this way, the days passed quickly.

One cold day, when the wind blew in even through the closed windows, the dog was lying in the middle of the room, his enormous mouth wide open. I came over, hoping to wake him and have him chase me, but he was sleeping deeply, so I settled down in front of him, my nose near his nose. I noticed how warm his breath was and how warm the world seemed to be near his mouth. I thought, What if I lie across his mouth? In it, so to speak. I won't bother his tongue. As usual, his tongue was hanging out of the side of his mouth. So I crept closer, and lay myself down across his enormous lower jaw.

The dog stirred and opened his eyes, which crossed when he tried to look at me. He sniffed once, and then twice, and then, convinced it was me lying in his mouth, and not some strange mouse or mole, he went back to sleep. Eventually, I turned over on my back and continued sleeping in the dog's warm mouth.

"Look at that," said the woman.

"That dog has the patience of a saint," said the man.

I was comfortable, very warm, and very wet when I awakened, and the dog slept on where he was. But since it was still chilly in this new house, I retreated to my new favorite place, behind the bright red woodstove in the living room.

When I first began to sleep beneath this stove, I inadvertently caused a great commotion. No one could find me, and I myself was so sound asleep, so happily stupefied by the heat, that I didn't hear the woman calling my name. I didn't hear her tap the dinner plate with a spoon, a sound that always brought me flying from behind my drawer, where I still periodically retreated.

Beneath the woodstove, the heat fell on me like a thick blanket, and it was as if I were once again in my wall, half buried beneath the warm body of my mother. Beneath that stove, I dreamed the most pleasant dreams. I felt myself grow warm until even my bones were warm, and my ears melted softly against my head, and, although I usually slept as a cat should, curled into a neat circle, when I rested beneath that stove, I sprawled out higgledy-piggledy, each paw pointing in a different direction. When my eyes opened, I staggered out, half melted, tilting this way or that way, stunned by the heat, and did not clean myself immediately because my fur was too hot against my tongue.

One day when I staggered out, I heard the woman and the man calling my name. *Foudini! Foudini!* They were going from room to room, calling me. Surely they could see me there, in the middle of the rug!

"Find the cat," they were telling the dog, who at that moment rushed down the stairs and stopped, his long nose pointing down at me.

"Where did you come from?" the woman asked. "We thought you were lost!"

"He must have a hiding place we don't know about," the man said, whereupon the dog sighed, and I understood that he had known where I was all along, and that while I slept, he had stood in front of the stove and whined and whimpered, but either the man and the woman didn't understand him or they couldn't see me when they bent down and looked beneath the stove. It is very dark beneath the stove, and except for the white lightning streak between my eyes, I am completely black.

Good, I thought. There, I am invisible. I will stay there the next time they begin to put boxes in the car.

The dog, of course, would do his best to give me away. I could already see that the dog, who loved me, loved the man and the woman more, because he would do whatever they asked him to do. When the woman tapped the sofa where she sat, the dog would jump up next to her and lay his long muzzle in her lap, and then she would pet him until he was quite drunk with happiness. At night, when she went to bed, the dog would leap up onto the bed with her, and finally settle down to sleep, laying his head across her ankles.

All this caused me to think. What was this petting for, and was it necessary, and did I have to put up with it? My mother had never petted me. She licked me and she nudged me with her head. I had no desire to be petted. At times, when I slept next to the dog, he would awaken and begin to lick me, and then he would lay an enormous paw across me, and no matter how I struggled, I could barely move. At times, the dog himself tried to pet me, but at the first stroke, I would be pinned to the ground.

But the woman was forever swooping down upon me, lifting me into the air, and settling me on her lap, and then she would try to pet me. I would sit still as long as I could stand it, and then I would get down from her lap and sit far away enough so that I was out of her reach. I would move to the couch and watch her, and this is what I saw.

She was always annoyed at me! She would often stare at me and blink and then blink again. Every cat is born knowing that blinking is a very bad sign indeed. Only an annoyed cat blinks at another cat. A happy cat stares with his eyes wide open. Since the woman was always blinking, I knew I displeased her, and a cat does not have to be a genius to know that an angry human being is a dangerous human being. Yet it was a puzzle. Annoyed as she always was, she still cooked my dinner and spoke nicely to me while I ate. At times, she succeeded in patting me on the head while I ate, and although I was afraid she would push my head right into the plate, I was so busy eating up my dinner that I didn't mind. But when I finished eating, I did mind.

I could see there would be a great deal to understand about my small world. The woman squinted and blinked at everyone, but I was the only one who seemed to mind or even to notice. I watched her as she stroked the dog's head and scratched him behind the ears. Blinking and more blinking. And yet the dog did not get up and move off. He showed no sign of alarm whatever. And then she and the man sat in chairs, and they blinked at each other while they talked, and neither of them jumped up and prudently sat across the room, watching each other from a safe distance. When I stared into the dog's eyes, even the dog blinked.

It was an annoyed world I lived in! At any moment, everyone might jump up and begin attacking everyone around him! At any instant, the woman might try to push the man down and stuff him into a box and throw him in the car! Although I was beginning to like the two human beings, I decided to keep my distance.

As soon as I made this decision, the woman redoubled her efforts to seize me, to pet me, and to carry me about, and when she did this, the dog would whine and glare unhappily at me, and when I jumped down from a chair, or from the couch, he would chase me about.

Every day the dog went out and chased small animals across the meadow. One day he went out and came back in dripping wet. I smelled frog and fish on his fur, and when he slept, I would press up close to him, hoping to see whatever he saw when he was sleeping. Sometimes it worked, and then I saw myself walking across the meadow, and the grass seemed far away, and my feet seemed very far below me, and when I opened my mouth to speak, a thundering roar came from my throat.

But he was most peculiar when it came to the car.

I hated the car. It smelled of misery and trips to the hospital and hours in a small blue box. It took us from our house in the city to the house in the country, and then, when we were happily settled into the country house, it took us back again. But if the dog saw the man and the woman walk toward the car, he would begin crying and whining and finally barking. He would throw himself against the wall of the car and paw at the door handle. Naturally I thought he was trying to attack the car and drive it off forever, but whenever the man or the woman opened the door, he would leap madly in, wag his tail, and press his wet nose to the window.

Finally, it occurred to me. He actually enjoyed riding in the car! Whenever he was outside and refused to come in, the woman would go to the car and open the door, and wherever he was, the dog would hear the sound of the car door opening, race back across the meadow, and leap into the car, and then they would grab him by the collar and drag him back into the house.

He was not farsighted, that dog.

One day I thought, I will sit with my head against the woman, and even though she blinks, I will sit still. But I would keep an eye on her. And that day, the woman stared into my eyes without blinking, not for long, but longer than usual. I became curious, and moved a little closer, until my head was on her thigh. She stared at me and didn't blink.

She was trying to befriend me. I saw that and decided to let her pet me, at least for a short time, and after a while fell asleep on the couch next to her, and when I opened my eyes, she was still petting me, the dog was glowering at me from the floor, and my fur was warm and smooth.

This is not so bad, I thought.

Grace interrupts now and asks, "Why is it they didn't let you out to run in the meadow? Why is it they don't let *me* out? What kind of life is this for a cat, born as we are with such sharp nails with which to defend ourselves, able to climb trees as quickly as a squirrel? The squirrels outside are so fat and conceited. They come to the window and wiggle their tails at us knowing we cannot come through the glass to get them. Other cats walk freely about in our yard! Pretty orange cats who sing to me when I sit on a shelf and watch them! They would play with me! I would like to play with them!"

I didn't know how to answer her. I know they will never let us out, and this is a great sadness, or was a great sadness, although today it is not. Today I am resigned. There was a time when I lurked at every door that opened, hoping to escape into the meadow to hunt the mice and moles and chipmunks who ran through the wet grass, scenting it with their vivid odors, aromas that drifted in even through the screens on the windows. I wanted to go with the dog on his trips to the stream. I wanted to climb trees and drop down onto the dog's unsuspecting head. I wanted to hide in piles of leaves and see if he could find me. I wanted to leap onto a stone in the stream and swat a fish up out of the water. I wanted to roll over and over in the grass and jump up and chase the large orange-and-black butterflies I saw fluttering through the air from my eternal window. I wanted to be waiting for the mole when it came up out of its burrow. I wanted to find a beautiful cat of my own, and wait for the day when she would carry my kittens out to me.

But the woman was afraid something would happen to us, and she believed—she still believes—that she could not bear it. She has seen city cats killed by other cats. She has seen cats die beneath the wheels of cars, cats and dogs struck down in the middle of the street by speeding cars, a cat poisoned by the neighbor next door. She has seen country cats frozen by the cold, cold nights. She says these things will not happen to us, and so she keeps us safe by keeping us indoors. And it is not a bad life, is it? We are loved; we are cared for; we are kept safe.

I did have my one adventure outside with the dog, and no one is likely to forget it. But I will not tell Grace about that, not yet. If she knew I had been out and she had not, she would begin plotting her own escapes into the out-side world, and she might not be as lucky as I was. After all, when I made my escape, the dog was still here. Now he is not.

When the dog left and did not come back, the woman saw how I turned my back to the room and slept on the sofa all day as if I were the one who had died, and so she hunted for little Grace and brought her here for me. I am glad she did it. Without little Grace, I would have gone on lying on the couch until I could no longer breathe in and out. But Grace is here, and even though I have my complaints about her, life is once again interesting and good.

The man and the woman go out every day and hunt for mice, not the kind of mice little Grace and I would find for ourselves, but mice that come chopped up in cans or in little glass jars. Sometimes the two of them leave the house for weeks, hunting food for us, and when they come back, they return with paper bags filled with canned mice. We are never hungry, and there is so much that makes me happy. Yet when I see little Grace sitting at the window looking out at her birds, or when I sit at the window and look out at the cats climbing our fence and dropping down into another garden, I feel a sadness that makes my head heavy and my paws slow. I jump down and find a safe place and go to sleep, and when I wake up, I feel better.

I am not merely resigned. I have grown into this life as a housecat, a housecat who lives sometimes in the city and sometimes in the country, and today I am a happy cat, but this happiness has come with age and experience. I know it is hopeless to explain this right now to little Grace, who sits at the window and sees an entire edible, deliciously sniffable world on the other side.

Instead, I decide to tell her a story from my own life. I say, Little Grace, the outside world is not always such a wonderful place.

Grace looks at me, narrows her eyes, licks her paw, and says, "Nonsense." She asks me, "How would you know, you who have never been out?"

I lose my temper and tell her that she has not been listening. Didn't I tell her of my time in the wall with my mother?

"Oh," she says. "That was all so long ago. The world has changed. *Now* it is a wonderful place."

Why should I be surprised? Cats are willful and stubborn creatures. They do not like to learn from experience. They are optimists who say to themselves, *If the world is not a wonderful place today, tomorrow it will be transformed. Tomorrow is another day! What does tomorrow have to do with yesterday? Every day the entire world is created all over again. This may be the day when all bad things are erased. I cannot wait to get out into this day and see if the world has been made over as I want it to be.*

Then there are cats like me, the exceptions to the rule, the pessimists. Still, years of happiness have begun wearing my pessimism away, and every year, I shed more of it, as I shed my summer fur before the winter.

"Let me tell you what happened one day at Mouse House," I said, "when even though I could not go out, part of the outside decided to come in."

"Can it do that?" asked Grace, her ears standing up straighter. "Can animals come in? Birds and other cats?"

"Oh, yes, birds can come in," I said. "But it is not such a wonderful thing. Once in Mouse House, the stove door opened, and a bird flew into the room. The woman got it before we did, and she took it outside."

"Birds belong to us!" Grace said resentfully.

"Yes," I said, "but this particular bird flew madly into walls, and finally it flew so hard into a wall that it fell to the floor, and the woman wrapped it in a towel and put it outside. Really, little Grace, it is not good sportsmanship to eat a bird that has knocked itself silly flying into walls!"

"Oh, I don't know," said Grace, licking her other paw.

"There is a lot you don't know," I said.

"Tell me about how the outside came in," Grace said, twitching her tail excitedly.

"Don't get your hopes up too high," I said. "It is not a happy story."

"None of your stories are happy stories," she said grumpily. "Your life in a wall, the doctors in the hospital!"

She spoke with a certain contempt, you see, and I was unhappy to hear it, because I know she will have to discover unhappiness. Sooner or later, every one of us does. I will not be happy on the day she grows sadder and wiser.

"Well, tell your story," she said impatiently.

"We were in Mouse House, which you know very well," I said. "And as you also know, the man and woman

are very careful about doors. They shut the doors behind them when they go to the woodshed or when they
go out to the car."

"Everyone knows that," said Grace.

"Yes, but one day they forgot to shut the door to the
woodshed, and a woodchuck walked in, and he went
through the kitchen into the living room. The man and
the woman were not there. They had gone away in the
car, hunting for food. And I was still a young cat, even
younger than you are, Grace. I saw an animal that looked
like a pillow, dog colored—"

"Dog colored?" interrupted Grace.

"Black and white and gray and brown and tan, the
same color as Sam, my dog," I said. "My dog was half
wolf, you know. He was very ferocious. He didn't like
woodchucks at all. I didn't know better, and I thought it
would be fun to play with this new animal. But as soon as
I went near the woodchuck, it began to make odd noises
and its lips pulled back over its teeth. It began swiping at
me with its long claws, and I was so foolish that I danced
even closer to the pillowlike animal. Just then the dog
came down from upstairs and saw what was what. He
growled and barked. But the woodchuck must have been
deaf, because it began advancing on me, and I was too
frightened to move or run.

"When the dog saw that, he attacked the woodchuck,
and I finally saw why the dog had such enormous teeth.

He got the woodchuck by the fur on his back, but the woodchuck managed to turn himself around. He was about to bite Sam with *his* teeth, which were even more terrible than my dog's. I jumped up onto the little table near the window, and from there, I jumped down onto the woodchuck, and I dug my claws into his skull. The woodchuck was so surprised he turned away from the dog, trying to find me. Then the dog got him. My dog's teeth went deep into the woodchuck's throat, and the woodchuck screamed and lay still. We watched the woodchuck twitch in the middle of the living room rug. Blood poured out of his throat like water.

"The man and the woman came back. They saw the woodchuck lying in the middle of the rug, rushed over to us, and ran their hands up and down our fur and would not stop until they were certain the woodchuck had not injured us. Then they picked up the woodchuck and carried him outside. They never let us eat animals we kill, you know. If I kill a mouse and eat off his head, the woman screams, gets a napkin, carries the mouse outside, and then comes back and usually she says, 'Good cat, good cat,' but I am never sure. Does she mean it?

"When I was small, I caught four mice, lined them up in a neat row and counted them again and again. *Tap* for the first mouse, *tap* for the second mouse, *tap* for the third, *tap* for the fourth. Oh, how satisfying that was! How I congratulated myself on my good work! I was happier counting them than eating them, although I did eat their heads. Their heads are delicious, you know. There's no resisting them. But when the woman came downstairs, what did she do? She screamed and ran back upstairs. She called me until I also came up, and then she slammed the door behind us, and said, 'Good cat, good cat.' Well, we will sell our souls to hear that, won't we? *Good cat, good cat?*"

"Not me," said little Grace. "Tell me the story about the outside coming in."

"I just told you that story! The woodchuck *was* the outside coming in! The outside has big claws and sharp teeth and it was heavier and stronger than I was, so heavy and strong he might have killed my dog. It is not all leaping and sniffing out there, Grace! The woodchuck would have eaten *you*, Grace!"

Grace stretched out and flipped onto her back. No one would eat anything as beautiful and attractive as she! "I would like to go outside," she said. "I would watch out for woodchucks. Someday I will go out."

"Yes, someday," I said. "Someday we will both go out."

We would never go out. I knew that. But why should little Grace know that? In time, she would come to know it. In time, she wouldn't mind.

"And we will chase squirrels and butterflies," Grace said dreamily.

"Squirrels and butterflies and wild mice," I said. "We will chase all of those."

"All of those," Grace said sleepily, curling her tail about her and falling asleep.

As she slept, I thought back to the early days in the city house, and the first trips to Mouse House, and how long it took for me to trust the woman. I marveled at what patience she must have had. Even my own mother did not have such patience. If I tried to leave my wall when she believed it unwise for me to let myself be seen, she would come out, grab me by the back of my neck, and carry me back in, my paws dangling helplessly in the air, and if I again tried to escape her, she would swat me good and hard with her claws out. Once she dragged me quite a distance, so that I felt every pebble and every rough spot on the concrete.

When I first learned to rest my head on the woman's thigh, I was still suspicious of her and always ready to flee. Frequently, just as I had settled down to existence in Mouse House, just as I had come to think I would forever be able to melt myself beneath woodstoves, the woman would grab me up and pack me into my blue box, and we would go back to the city house, where there are no woodstoves, only heating vents in the floor. And so I remained suspicious of her.

But as time passed, I worried less and less about the blue box, and one day, we were once more in Mouse

House, and the woodstoves were warm, and snow flew against the windowpanes, and I was so happy that I began to prop myself against her thigh, so that my front paws, my shoulders, and my head rested on her. After several months of this, I managed to climb into her lap. And once in her lap, I made a lovely discovery. When the woman breathed in and out, I went gently up and down. This was like sleeping on my mother's stomach, only better. And when the woman held me close to her chest, I could hear her heart, *pound, pound, pound,* as my mother's heart used to beat, but slower and louder, the most wonderful and comforting sound. I would sleep deep sleeps and dream of thick woods, and sometimes of a place that was very hot, where the sun always shone and where huge stone cats stood guard over enormous buildings.

But then I would again be snatched up and again packed into the car, and we would go back to Cold House in the city, where there were few smells of wild creatures, just the occasional whiff of a mouse on his way from one house to another. The dog tried to tell me that these trips from one house to the other were part of our lives, but I did not believe it. I told him such long rides in a car, going from the city house to the country house, were not necessary. I told him my theory, which I still believe, that people do not know everything, because if they did, why would they talk into flat boxlike things they hold to their ear—as if they think such a box can really hear what they have to say? And why do they spend so much time staring at books, pieces of paper that are quite comfortable to lie upon, warmer in winter than a wood floor, but surely not interesting. Surely not as interesting as we are!

Clearly, people do not know everything, because if they did, they would not get in a car and drive around the world one hundred times over, simply to get from Cold House to Mouse House or Mouse House to Cold House. They would simply go through the door! Couldn't the dog see that? Even an idiot could see that!

"What door do you mean?" the dog asked me.

"The door that goes from Mouse House to Cold House," I said impatiently.

"And just where is this door?" the dog asked me.

"It is *somewhere* in the house," I said. "Probably in the attic behind some boxes. But the people are lazy and don't want to move the boxes in order to open the door. If they did, they would find Mouse House on the other side. If they opened the door, we could go through and find ourselves in the kitchen of Mouse House. It is as plain as the whiskers on your face."

"There is no such door," the dog insisted, "and you would do well to stop your piteous crying in the car, because they will get tired of you and will not give you bones to chew on."

Bones to chew on!

"You are as foolish as they are," I told the dog.

"Look here, Shorty," he said, "I keep my head out the window when we drive, and do you know why I do that?"

"To keep cool," I said.

"To smell all the smells along the way," said the dog. "There are smells that belong to every mile we drive over, and if, one day, the car should crash, I would be able to find my way back to either of the houses by my Map of Smells. Something is wrong with your nose, or your Map of Smells would tell you we go many miles before we get to Mouse House."

"And how do you know that?" I asked the dog. "How do you know that the man isn't driving in big circles? If you followed your Map of Smells, you would also go in a circle. You would exhaust yourself for no reason! When all you have to do is go through the door in one house and come out in the next house!"

"Well, there is no talking to you," said the dog. "Do all cats have such terrible noses?"

I said my nose was an excellent nose, and the dog was conceited about his nose because it was so large. The space between his nose and his eyes was as long as my body. "Even if I have a small nose," I said, "it works very well."

"It doesn't work at all," the dog said, "if you think we drive in circles. Will you stop that weeping in the car? It doesn't do you any good at all. All it does is give me a headache. And the woman must constantly talk to you. How can I listen to it, hour after hour! 'Foudini. Don't worry, Foudini. We'll be there soon.' What an idiot she must think you are, to repeat the same thing so many times!"

"And I suppose you're not an idiot?" I asked the dog. "Every time it rains, whenever it thunders, you jump into the bathtub and hide your head beneath the faucet. You try so hard to get under beds that you lift the beds into the air. Such a big dog, to be afraid of thunder and lightning!"

While we argued, I had been lying cozily next to the dog, but he became exasperated when I called him an idiot, and he picked up his enormous paw and pinned me to the ground.

"Little cats should listen to their elders," he said. "In my dreams, I am running through fields, and when I come to a stone fence, I leap over it, and then I am in the dark woods where the earth is soft with fallen pine needles and the deer cannot hear me coming, and I know I will catch the deer, and all the wolves in my pack will eat well. The sky darkens and the moon disappears and the stars vanish and I can see nothing at all, but it doesn't matter, because I have my Map of Smells and I continue on my way after the deer.

"But then a terrible thing happens! But then the lightning flashes, and as it lights everything up, I see it come down from the sky and strike my father, who lies down stiff and silent. I stay with him and howl and howl, trying to wake him again, and the storm passes. The sun comes out, and rays of gold light slice through the trees above me. But he will not wake up, and eventually his smell begins to change, and I know he is a dead thing, and when I know he is no longer a wolf, I understand that I have to leave him. And I know that the lightning has taken away his wolf-smell and changed him into something terrible. When the sky barks with thunder, I know I must go and hide myself. Perhaps you don't dream very well either," the dog said.

"No cat has ever been struck by lightning," I said, and the dog said, "Dream again! Cats climb trees and lightning strikes trees! Once lightning struck a tree in front of Mouse House and knocked it to the ground, and when it fell, it broke a window with one of its arms."

"I will stay out of trees in lightning storms," I said, thinking it over.

But the dog said I must do better than that. When I hear the sky begin to bark, he said, I must hide myself as well as possible, preferably beneath something heavy, so the lightning will not see me.

"The lightning has good eyes," he said. "As good as yours."

I pointed out that the man and the woman did not hide themselves when they heard the sky begin to bark and flash, and the dog said that, as I myself had pointed out, human beings did not know everything, and he was sure human beings were struck down every time lightning flashed in the sky.

"But the woman sits in a chair and watches the storm with me in her lap," I said, and the dog said I was foolish to allow it. Moreover, when was I going to stop calling our two people the man and the woman? Wasn't it about time I gave them names? *He* had given them names dog years ago. I asked him what names he had given them, and he said that I must think up my own names. Dogs thought up names for their people, but he thought only an unwise dog would tell anyone what those secret names were. I said if he told me their names, I would call them by the same names. But the dog refused. He said the names he gave our people were his own business, and it was my business to think up my own.

And so I decided to find good and proper names for our people.

At the time I decided to give them names, things had reached such a pass that I would spend hours lying on the woman's stomach. I would spend hours in her lap while she typed and typed, another mysterious activity that accomplished nothing but caused little letters of light to crawl buglike across the screen of her machine. I had long since come to resent that machine because the woman paid so much attention to it for so long. One day while I was lying in her lap watching her type, I sat up and put my paw on the keys, and rows and rows of *j*'s began flying back and forth across the screen. When I picked up my paw, the letters stopped. When I put my paw back on the keys, more and more *j*'s flew across the screen.

This is a boring business, I thought.

"Will you look at that?" said the woman, and she called to the man to come in. "He types rows and rows of *j*'s," she said. "Isn't that marvelous?"

"If I were you," the man said, "I'd lock that cat out of my room when I was working."

Lock me out! Lock out *that cat!* What did he mean, referring to me in such a way?

I do not like that man, I thought. That man is jealous of me.

Just lately, I had begun sleeping in bed with the woman. I would start out with the dog at the foot of the bed, and then the sound of the woman's breathing would tempt me, and I would slowly move upward until I was right next to her. I would put my head down on the pillow, press my nose into her cheek, and fall asleep. At first, the woman's breathing made it difficult to sleep, because when she breathed out, the little winds of her nose struck my ears and caused them to twitch. But I soon learned where on the pillow my head should be, and then the sound of her breathing was as pleasant and reassuring as the waves of warmth that washed over me when I slept beneath the woodstove.

Gradually, when I reached the pillow, the woman's eyes would flicker open, and she would lift up her blanket and cover me with it, and I would not struggle trying to free myself. After more time passed, I saw the advantages of moving even closer to the woman, because then I was warm all over, and when I did this, the woman would put her arm over me, and I would fall asleep, purring. It was warm and hummy in that bed, and at the foot the dog snored loudly in his sleep. I asked myself how I could be more happy.

But of course even this happiness had its unhappy side, because when the man, who went to bed later than the woman, came in and found me lying on his side of the bed, he would put his large hand beneath me and move me over as if he were a spatula and I were an egg in a frying pan. He would say, Stupid cat, and thump his pillow about. Naturally, I did not want to sleep next to him, so I would go back to the foot of the bed and sleep against the dog, who would begin to purr as soon as he felt me arrive, and if he was still awake, he would turn his head toward me and lick me once with his tongue, and so I would fall asleep, my back warm against the dog's rough fur, my recently licked side damp and cold, but warming quickly.

One night while I was pressed up against the dog, listening to his rumbly breathing, and the breathing in and out of the man and woman, the names they should have suddenly appeared to me. I will call the woman Warm, I decided, and I will call the man Pest.

It is obvious why I decided to call the woman Warm. She was always talking to me or carrying me or attaching strings to paper balls or bringing me little sacks stuffed with catnip. Or she was trying to brush me—that was not so nice. The bristles of the brush scraped my skin, and without thinking, I would attack the brush handle, and I often miscalculated and scratched the woman's hand instead, and then she would cry out and I would be filled with remorse. But almost always—except when she packed me—she was lovely.

And the man was Pest because when he climbed into our bed, he would say things about "my side of the bed" and "Aren't I entitled to a little space of my own?" Or "Can't you keep the cat on your side?" and "Do you think that cat has fleas? I've been itching lately." However, he did cook for us. When he got up, he would go to the kitchen and take meat from the refrigerator and heat it up in a pan, while the woman would only open a can or a jar.

But he preferred the dog to me; that was clear enough. The dog slept on the rug in back of his office chair, and when it began to rain, the dog crept beneath his desk and lay across his feet.

As I thought about it, it became clear: every animal has his Assigned Person. I was assigned to Warm. The dog was assigned to Pest. The dog and I were assigned to one another. Really, the world was orderly after all.

When I fell asleep, I thought, I must tell Grace that we each have our Assigned Person. She must pick someone and follow him about the house and sit on his lap, not scatter herself about as if she were confetti, as she now does. Grace believes the entire world is assigned to *her*. It is wrong of me to let her dance through life in such ignorance.

After I carefully and patiently explained everything, Grace would, I knew, assign herself to Pest. She is the kind of cat who gives other cats a reputation as ravenous ingrates who will sell their souls for a warm plate of food. She falls in love immediately with whoever feeds her, although usually she has the good sense to stay away from Warm. I will put up with almost anything from Grace the Cat, but I will not let her take my place with Warm. Warm's lap is assigned to me. And so Grace sleeps on the footstool next to Warm's feet, because when she does this, she knows I will not glare and chase her.

All the same, she has her eye on Warm. Yesterday, she sat in Warm's lap, and when I glared at her, she closed her eyes and pretended to be asleep, although she was watching me, as I well knew, through slitted eyes. At night, when she climbs up on the bed, she pretends to sleep soundly at the foot of the bed, but when she thinks I am asleep she begins creeping up toward the pillows.

When I pick up my head and turn to look at her, she thinks better of it and goes back. But she is encroaching. Grace the Cat is an encroaching sort of cat.

Lately she has been trying to teach Warm to speak! She stands on a counter and speaks to her, and Warm speaks back in a cat voice. It is a good and authentic cat voice, but naturally Warm does not know what she is saying, and so the two of them have the most extraordinary conversations. "I smell a squirrel," Warm says, when what she means to say is *Are you hungry again?* Or she says, for no reason whatever, "Fly soup!" or "Bird feathers! Go away!" And if Grace asks her, "Why won't you open that cabinet so I may go in and hunt for mice?" Warm replies, "Twitchy whiskers! Danger!"

"Have that muffin?" Grace asks. "Have that fish? Have that mouse?"

"Male cat smell!" says Warm.

"Have that ham?" says Grace.

"Alarm! Alarm!" says Warm.

They are a tower of babble, those two.

When Warm speaks to me, I don't encourage her by answering. When I was a small cat, I was occasionally tempted into trying to talk to her, but the resulting nonsense made my head spin, and today if I want something—a bite to eat, or to be let out of a room or into one, or to summon Warm, who will rescue me from Grace when she is seized by one of her affection fits and uncontrollably bites at my ears—I call out in a loud voice and turn a deaf ear to Warm's execrable attempts at Cattish.

Warm will never learn to speak it. You would think this would be clear to her, but it isn't, because whenever she mews at a cat she sees on the street, or whenever she mews at Grace, the startled animal always stops and looks about for another cat, and so Warm believes cats can understand her. She has no idea the cat on the street has just heard someone say, "Goldfish! In the trees! Squirrel milk! The egg is coming! Ear thorns! Collar food!"

When she takes me to the doctor's office, I apologize profusely to the other cats in the room, saying, "She doesn't mean it. She doesn't know what she's saying."

"Dog's breath!" says Warm.

And the other cats regard me with pity, asking themselves why I am so unfortunate as to be assigned to a human being who is a complete lunatic. It goes without saying that I cannot put up with their attitude. I am a loyal cat. I cannot sit by and let perfectly strange cats insult Warm, and so I struggle out of Warm's arms and attack the cat who has had such dreadful things to say about her. But am I rewarded? I am not. Warm catches me up, packs me back in my box, and scolds me through the grating. "Now," she says, "they will all believe you are still a vicious, crazy cat." And then she turns to the cat I've just attacked, and says, "Fur ball tongue! Food fur!" It is enough to make one weep, how Warm murders the language.

But I was speaking of the days when I was still young and still assigned to my dog.

We cats cannot contemplate anything—unless that thing is a possible mouse—for very long. Our attention leaps from this to that, from past to present. We look at the world and struggle to understand it, and the struggle is so difficult, we go to sleep and take our famous naps. And while we sleep, we dream our dreams of past lives and past generations of cats, and sometimes when we awaken, we have the answer to the question that so exhausted us and caused us to close our eyes.

I remember that for some time I was obsessed by the weather.

I was born in the winter, as I said, and so I thought it would always be winter and the furnace would always be on, roaring in the basement, and the pipes would always be hot and wonderful to sleep upon, but then, without my noticing it, the house grew warmer and warmer. I thought the furnace had been staying awake longer and breathing harder, but one day the entire house was hot, windows were opened up wide, and when I listened for the furnace's voice, I could not hear it.

Suddenly, my good suit of fur was too heavy for me, and I was happy when the dog licked me with his great tongue and made me cooler than before.

"What is this?" I asked the dog. "Why is our fur too warm for us?" And the dog looked at me and said lazily, "This is the spring. It will be worse in the summer."

He told me to go to the window and I would see little flowers growing around the tree, and in the trees I would see many birds who were not there when I first came to live in the house. I went to the window and looked out. There were the flowers and their sweet smells and the birds, singing songs I had never before heard. "You see?" the dog asked me. "It is spring. Sometimes it is very hot in the spring." And he lay on his side, panting.

"Tell them to turn off the heat," I said. "Bark for all you are worth."

"They have nothing to do with it," the dog said. "Time passes, and the heat, which is a gold dog, attacks the cold, a white dog, and the gold dog gets him by the throat, and the white dog runs away until his throat is healed. When his throat is healed, then it will be cold again."

"No!" I shouted. "None of these fairy dog tales! It is that button over there on the wall! Get up on your hind legs and turn that button, and it will again be cold!"

The dog sighed and growled low in his throat, meaning to say that once I got an idea in my head, there was no getting it out.

I said I wouldn't put up with it, the house was like a pot on a stove, we would all be cooked, I was going to complain, I wouldn't eat when they put food before me, I wouldn't sleep on the bed, no one could pet me, I would tear my collar from my neck, I would shriek when I was brushed, I would go back beneath the bookcase, I wouldn't come out, no matter how often they called me.

"Go ahead," said the dog. "You will be a thin and hot cat. And," he said, "I don't believe you will fit beneath the bookcase any longer. You are becoming a heavy cat. When you walk on my side, I think, That cat is so heavy he must be made of stone."

"But the button!" I cried. "Up there on the wall!"

"It is the button up in the sky you have to worry about. These are the lazy days. I would like them except—"

"Except what?" I demanded. If something worse was to come, I wanted to know what it was.

"Oh," said the dog, scratching his muzzle with his paw, "nothing. Nothing at all."

"It can't be worse than this," I said mournfully.

"Absolutely not, no, certainly not," said the dog, not very convincingly. "But the first time is a shock. If you'd been born in the summer, think how angry you'd be when the snow began to fall."

"Snow is supposed to fall! People are supposed to shiver and cover themselves with blankets! We are supposed to crawl beneath the covers and sleep with them!"

"Well, all that is over for a while," the dog said, lazily stretching himself out in a patch of light.

I soon found ways of keeping myself cool. I could, for example, jump into the bathtub and lie upon its cool white bottom. Or I could sit beneath the faucet and let drops of cold water drip onto my head and shoulders, or retreat to the wonderful basement that was cool and even chilly, although in the winter it had been so warm. And after a while, I came to think that spring and summer were not such bad things, because it was pleasant to lie still and let your bones melt and dream that you were once more at the bottom of a heap of other small cats, licked by the warm, sunlike tongue of your mother.

And so I informed the dog that the spring and summer were not such bad times after all, and perhaps it was not a bad idea (I was not ready to say it was a *good* idea) that there were such things as different seasons and different smells. Now, for example, it was pleasant to sit in the kitchen window and watch the birds fight for a place on the sticks of the bird feeder and to feel a soft breeze stir my fur just as it stirred the new, bright green grass. And it was interesting to watch all manner of things floating down through the air, lovely yellow-green things that looked like green snow and fell slowly, twirling in the air as snowflakes had twirled in the winter. Then, as was frequently the case in those days, I began to feel sorry for myself because I could not go outside and inspect these green, spirally things.

"If that's all you want," said the dog, "I can easily take care of that when I go outside. I'll roll over and over, and the green things will stick to my fur, and when I come back in, you can pick them out with your tongue."

He said this so casually; he took it so for granted that he was allowed into the wide world while I was not, that I was quite annoyed. "But if you can go out, why can't I go out with you?" I asked him, and he said that he was large, as I had perhaps noticed, and there was no place in the fence he could squeeze through, so he had to remain in the yard. Whereas a cat could easily climb a fence and drop down on the other side, and there were many, many places that I with my elastic and compressible body could squeeze through, and there were many trees I could climb whose branches overhung the neighboring gardens, and from them I could drop down into a neighbor's unfamiliar grass. "Besides, you use a litter box while I require a bigger place. Naturally," he said, "they know I can take care of myself if it comes to it."

"I have sharp claws!" I said, and as if to answer all my objections and put an end to my prideful boasting, which he knew had only begun, the dog stood over me so that the wide expanse of his stomach was like a ceiling, and he slowly lowered himself onto me, and of course I could not move. "It would take me two seconds to break your neck," he said, "and two minutes to chew you to pieces. A smaller dog would do almost as well."

"But if I was careful and stayed out of sight! If I climbed a tree whenever a dog approached!"

"Our people will not take such chances," the dog said, and I asked him if he didn't agree that it was unfair. Didn't he think I should be allowed out with him? He shook his head sadly and said, "I myself have killed cats—before I knew better. It was not hard. No, if it were up to me, you would not go out either."

"You would keep me in?"

"Certainly," he said.

Just then, Warm called to him, and while I watched from the kitchen, she opened the back woodshed door, and keeping her eye on me, she let him out and closed the door firmly behind him, and when he came back in, I was too angry to speak to him. He settled himself on the Victorian sofa he had chosen for himself, and I jumped up onto the leather sofa, turned my back to the room, and went to sleep.

But I have never been able to remain angry long, and when I awakened and found the dog standing in front of my couch, green things in his fur, I immediately forgave him for leading a more fortunate life than my own.

"I can bring you more of these," the dog said, "when I next go out."

"They are not bugs at all. They are only parts of trees," I said, disappointed.

"Of course they are parts of trees," said the dog. "Do you want a bug? I can carry one in to you in my mouth."

I didn't want a bug, but I did want a squirrel, and I asked him if he would mind bringing one back for me the next time he went out. But at this the dog looked sad and said that he had chased squirrels for the ten years he had been alive, and had never once gotten close enough to catch one between his teeth.

"Oh, you don't know how to hunt," I said, because I had watched him often enough through the window. "You dash after everything the instant you see it, and a squirrel is faster and can run through the very smallest places, and he can leap into a tree and disappear over the roofs of garages before you've taken two steps. I will teach you to hunt," I said, and I lay down on the rug and flattened myself, and said, "This is how you must crouch down. And then you must wait until the animal finds something it wants to eat and is no longer paying attention to you, and when he is chewing and happy, you must inch forward on your belly, and at the last minute, you must pounce. Believe me, this works. I have seen my mother do it."

"Your tail is twitching," the dog said. "The squirrel will see your tail twitching."

"If I were outside waiting for the squirrel, my tail would not twitch," I said.

"Your tail always twitches," the dog said. "That's how I know when you're about to pounce on me."

"My tail does not always twitch!"

"It does."

"And the squirrel wouldn't see my tail! My nose would be pointed at him."

"A squirrel up in the tree would see your tail twitch and warn the squirrel you're hunting!"

"I'd hide myself in the leaves!" I said.

We began to argue, and I lost patience and tried to hit the dog on the nose, and he tried to grab me by the tail, and then he chased me through the house, and after he was finished, I chased him until both of us were tired out.

"It is warm and nice," I said, as we lay in front of the living room window in a pool of yellow light. "Summer and spring are not so bad."

"Hmmmph," said the dog, and it seemed to me his eyes were full of worry.

Then one day Pest came down the steps, and he carried two odd, gray boxes with him. They are going to pack me, I thought. I watched the dog, because if he jumped up and began crying with eagerness, I would

70

wait for my chance and escape into the basement and hide myself in the rafters. Last time I was packed, I was caught because Warm blocked the hole cut out of the basement door, and so when I cleverly ran past her as she took a pot from the stove, I was shocked to find myself facing a wooden board held in place by two heavy bricks. It is not so easy to outwit these humans, I thought. They plan ahead. I must outplan them.

But when the dog saw these gray boxes, he did not leap excitedly about. He did not jump on the couch and put his paws up on its rim while he looked out the window at the driveway. He looked at the gray boxes and began to whine, and then he lay down on the rug and put his paws over his nose and continued to whimper.

Were they going to pack *him?*

But they had never packed him before.

When I asked him what those boxes were for, he only whimpered louder, and I saw he refused to look at them again.

Warm came over and lay one box down on its side and began to open it, and I ran up the steps and watched from the safety of the landing. I didn't like the look of it, a huge box with no grating in its walls.

It was a box full of Warm's clothes! And it *was* full. I didn't think there would be enough room in that box for me, but all the same, I was frequently packed, so it was unwise to take chances.

Finally, I heard Warm going down to the basement, and then I crept back down the steps and looked at the gray box. There were Warm's sweaters and skirts. There was her hairbrush, the one she sometimes used to brush me. There was her shiny bottle of summer smells.

I stepped carefully into the box. It might be possible to fit me in. But there were no holes in the lid of this box. How would I breathe? Then I thought, It is a very big box. Perhaps they intend to pack the dog after all.

It was worse than I thought, worse than I could have imagined, because one day Warm and Pest carried the boxes out onto the front porch, and from the front porch, they carried them into a strange car driven by someone I had never before seen, and the car drove off with them, and the daylight faded, and night came, and still Warm and Pest did not return to the house.

Instead, three young men came into the house and began to jabber to one another, and one pointed at me and laughed, saying I was too fat, and another one pointed to the dog and said he needed to go out for more walks, and when it was time for our dinner, they did not cook up our usual fragrant and chewy meat, but instead set a dish in front of us filled with things that looked as if they had once lived in a garden. There were white chunks that looked like cheese but were not cheese, and I thought, I will not eat whatever this is. I will wait until

Warm and Pest come back to feed me as I am accustomed to being fed.

But the dog went over to his dish and ate everything on his plate, and then lay down sadly in front of the door.

Where was Warm? Where was Pest? And what were these three people doing in our house? I should drive them off! The dog should jump on one of them and knock him down and growl and bite his chin and make them all flee the place! But when I told this to the dog, he only looked at me sadly, went over to my dish, looked at me questioningly as if to say *Won't you eat this?* and when I twitched my tail and narrowed my eyes, meaning I had no intention of even licking at such repulsive food, the dog sighed and with one swipe of his tongue cleared my plate.

I will wait for Warm, I thought again. She always comes back. Sometimes she and Pest go out and come back late at night. They will come back later. When they come back, she will see these people who are foolish enough to think they can live in our house. Our house? Our nest! Once she knows they are here, she will throw them out. I settled myself on a windowsill and stared out, looking for signs of Warm, but no one came to the door, no key rattled in the lock, no familiar footsteps woke me from my dream when I fell asleep.

She will come back soon, I told myself, listening for telltale sounds, but there was only one bird calling to another bird, the wind in the thick green leaves, a car speeding past but not stopping, and, far away, a dog barking in a shrill voice, as if frightened.

When I next opened my eyes, the light had returned, and my stomach was empty and growling. One of the men came down and put another plate of garden things and white chunks before me, but I again refused to eat it. Warm would be back any minute!

But she did not come back.

The dog lay on the kitchen floor and did not move. He watched me as I jumped from the table to the window.

"Where are they?" I asked him.

"They will not come back," he said.

Not come back! Never? Had they gone out to hunt and disappeared forever, as my mother had done?

"This happens every summer when the weather turns hot," the dog said. "You must eat, or you will not be here when they come back."

"When will they come back?" I asked. "Where do they go?"

"I don't know where they go," the dog said. "When they come back, their clothes are full of strange smells that belong nowhere on my Map of Smells. It is a mystery, where they go. They will come back when the heat begins to leave."

"And who are these three new people!" I cried.

"They will live here and feed us and take me out for walks," the dog said.

"But I don't want them here!"

The dog looked at me sadly. "And how would you open our cans? We would have no canned meat to eat, and we would starve."

"I would hunt for mice!" I said. "We can drink water from the toilet bowl! Attack them! Make them leave!"

"It is no use," the dog said. "Eat when they feed you." He laid his head on his paw and closed his eyes. I jumped down from the window and swatted at his tail. Perhaps he was exaggerating. How did he know Warm wouldn't be back? I swatted at his tail again. We might as well chase one another through the house. But the dog sighed deeply and would not move.

Day succeeded day, and still Warm and Pest did not come. Gradually, I began to eat the garden food. But I did not like the three men. They had begun to work at sawing up something on the front porch. Their saws made screaming noises. And when they came back in and petted me, their hands were too heavy, and afterward my back ached. The dog was quiet and gloomy and refused to chase me, and I saw that the world had come to an end.

One day, I went down into the basement, climbed up on a furnace pipe, and went to sleep. I stayed there until

I heard the click of my tin plate against the kitchen floor, and then I went up to eat, and afterward I went back down again. My fur was growing dusty and clotted because no one brushed me, and my paws were dirty because it was too much trouble to wash them.

I lost all track of time. I slept on the pipes and dreamed and forgot about the dog. I never thought about him until dinnertime, when I found him sadly chewing his dinner next to my plate. Before I returned to the basement, I would go to the window and listen for Warm and Pest, but they never came. I ate and ate and I slept and slept and I grew fatter and fatter until I could barely jump from the floor to the chair and from the chair to the windowsill. My lavender collar grew tight, but there was no one to loosen it.

They are gone forever, I thought. They will never come back. They will not come back when the heat leaves. The dog says they will, but he is trying to cheer me up. He is so sad he does not believe it himself. From now on, I will dream in the basement and wait for my nine lives to use themselves up.

I am being punished, I thought. But what have I done?

That night, as I lay in the rafters, the stone cats of my dream came to visit me, and they told me that they had not always been made of stone, but had been turned to stone as a punishment.

"And will I be turned to stone?" I asked them, and they said they didn't know, because they didn't know what it was I had done wrong, and I said I didn't know either.

"Did you forget to protect your queen?" a stone cat asked.

I told him that I did not have a queen, only a woman named Warm and a man named Pest, both of whom had gone off in a strange car, taking two large gray boxes with them, and now I was fed terrible food and no one petted me properly, no one said, *Oh, good cat, oh, nice cat, you are my favorite cat.* No one sang my special song to me at night when I got into bed. And I never got into bed anymore because there was someone new in the bed, and he was not Warm or Pest, and he laughed at me because now that I had grown so fat I made so much noise when I jumped down from my chair, and so I slept in the basement in the dusty rafters, still waiting, although I no longer knew for what.

"Waiting you no longer know for what," said the stone cat with a sigh. "We have been doing that for centuries."

"What were you before you were turned to stone?" I asked, and the biggest of the stone cats said, "It is a long story, but I will tell it to you. Once we were beautiful cats, as you are beautiful, and because we were beautiful, everyone adored us, and we were given the best fish to eat, and cushions were placed about palace rooms for us to sleep on, and dogs were beaten if they dared chase us, and we were brushed and combed and even bathed in warm water.

"Mice were caught for us and placed in front of our pillows, their hearts still beating, and we ate them, and the queen wore a headdress made of feathers, and next to her seat, which she called a throne, she kept a special feather, and she would make that feather run along the ground teasingly or jump into the air, and we would run after it and leap after it, and so she played with us both in her palace and on her boat.

"And on the boat were fishermen who caught fresh fish for us, and so we were always happy to be taken aboard. There was little we had to do, only one thing. If anyone approached the queen with evil intentions, we were to warn her by our loud hissing, and if she failed to be warned, and if the evil one moved closer to her, we were to throw ourselves at his feet and claw at his legs, or climb up on the armrests of her great throne and throw ourselves at his face and claw out his eyes. And we did not mind this. We were good at this, because, as you know, cats like to fight, and it is in a cat's nature to protect those he loves.

"And more than one of us died protecting the queen. Oh, yes, my own mother and father died protecting the queen. My father died after attacking the queen's father, who only wanted to play with his daughter, but my father thought the old king meant her some harm, and so he did his duty, and so my father was put to death. But my mother died the more horrible death, and the way she died was not uncommon.

"One day, the cook brought the queen a dish of wonderful spiced meat, and the queen was about to begin eating, when my mother smelled the unmistakable aroma of poison, and so she jumped onto the queen's lap and knocked her plate to the floor. And the queen could not understand why she had done this and shouted at her! And so my mother jumped down and took several bites of the food, and then climbed back up into the queen's lap, and only a few minutes later, her whiskers drooped and she began to writhe and froth at the mouth, and soon she twitched all over, and then she lay still and never moved again.

"*Then* the queen understood that her food had been poisoned, and she ordered her stone carvers to build a statue of my mother, and that statue was carved out of hard, black stone, and placed in her garden among all the other statues.

"But a time came when we grew less vigilant. Perhaps we had grown too playful and too accustomed to the worshipful way we were treated. We are lazy animals, after all. The people had begun to say we were gods, and we believed them. A cat can always be talked into accepting a compliment! But even if we were more indolent, we still drove off those with evil intentions. We still tasted the queen's food when its aroma displeased us. But who could have foreseen that the queen would become her own enemy? And if we had foreseen it, would we have known what to do?

"When we were appointed protectors of the queen, no one told us that the queen herself might become her own most dangerous enemy. We didn't know that people could administer poison to themselves. But this is what happened.

"One day, the queen, who had been growing more and more unhappy, came into her throne room with a sly look. We all observed that look, but we didn't understand its meaning. We saw her carry in a basket and set that basket beneath her feet, but we thought nothing of it. The queen often had a basket with her, and in it she carried her bright jewels or a little wooden pipe which she put in her mouth and touched with her fingers until it played lovely songs.

"This time, when the queen reached into her basket, we could not see what she took from it. We did see her raise her cupped hands to her throat, but again we thought nothing of it. But this time she had a small, green, poisonous snake in her hands, and when the snake bit her, the queen smiled at us, stiffened, and did not move again.

"We were heartbroken, because just as we had been

the queen's protector, so was she our protector. And we were blamed for her death! Everyone assumed that someone had brought the deadly snake to the queen and that we were too lazy or cowardly to stop him. No one understood us when we said that the queen herself had held the snake against her own throat. It had been so long since people and cats spoke the same language, as they once did, long ago, which is why, even now, a human being can mew like a cat, and the cry of a newborn infant is the same as the sound of a cat's crying.

"Everyone turned on us. And the sorcerer came, and he called the palace cats together and unrolled a parchment from which he read, and as he read, we felt ourselves growing heavier and colder, and it seemed to us that the ground had fallen away beneath us and that we looked down on our world from a great height.

"And that is how we were turned to stone. And now we can move only when a living cat dreams, and we can move only in that cat's dreams, but our bodies are stone and remain behind us in that hot land you dreamed of once before, and as soon as you stop dreaming, we must return to our stone bodies and stay in them staring out across the gold sands until another cat begins to dream and so calls us up."

"And will you come to any cat who dreams?" I asked.

The stone cat said no; he and the other stone cats only

came to other cats who were sorrowful and in danger of losing their lives.

"Am I in danger of losing my life?" I asked, and the cat said I was. I must get down from the rafters and walk and take an interest in the mice that freely ran about in the basement while I slept.

"There have been other cats here before you," the stone cat said. "Surely you know that. Surely you have picked up their scent."

"Yes," I said. "There were other cats before me. What were they like?"

"There was a little black cat named Emily, and she was a great protector. When she and her kittens were taken sneezing to the hospital, a doctor picked up one of her kittens, who cried out. And she leaped from the table and sunk her claws into the doctor's chest, and he asked your Assigned Person, 'Is this cat always so vicious?' When in fact Emily the Cat was not vicious at all.

"So you see you have been preceded by some very remarkable cats. Emily the Cat lived to be twenty, and one of her kittens lived to be nineteen, and even when he was nineteen, she would not let him go upstairs alone, because the dog who lived here in those days hated cats and might have harmed him. And when that kitten had grown into an old cat who was every day growing weaker, she lay on the top of those basement steps with her head on his back, and stayed there until he no longer moved. And your human being was surprised, because she thought Emily the Cat was the one who was sick because she was older and she never moved. She thought the kitten—well, he was a very old kitten by then—was the one staying with his mother to comfort her. So you see, even today cats are protectors and have their work cut out for them, and you will have your own job to do, and you will not be able to do it if you are so fat that you hurt your four ankles whenever you jump down from a chair."

"But Warm is gone, and Pest is gone," I said, "and they will not come back. Whom am I to protect? The only one left to me is the enormous dog who lives upstairs."

"I don't think he is the one you are meant to protect," the stone cat said, and as he spoke, he began to grow shimmery, and I could see the walls of the basement through his body. "But there will be someone you are meant to protect. There always is. We never knew we would have to protect the queen's throat from the queen's own hand." He was wavering and shimmering, and I knew he would soon be gone, just as I knew he had come before, and when I opened my eyes and was again awake, I would have forgotten his visit. "Will you come again?" I asked him, and he said he didn't know. He only came to good and worthy cats, and he had come to me after I threw myself upon the head of the woodchuck who had attacked my dog. Did I remember?

I did.

"You must wait for Warm even if she doesn't come back," he said. "Because if she does come back and doesn't find you, wherever you have gone, you will turn to stone. She is the human being to whom you are assigned. Your dog told you that, and your dog was right."

And I decided in my heart that I would wait for her even if I used up all my nine lives waiting.

But days passed, and still she did not come.

It was so hot. I began to search for the coolest places, and finally I thought I had found what I wanted. It was very cool on top of the square white washing machine that made noise all winter. I took to lying on top of it.

One day, the door to the machine was open.

It must be even cooler inside, I thought. I jumped in through the machine's round door.

"Get out of there!" said my dog, who had come looking for me. "Right away! That is a dangerous machine! You'll be drowned!"

"It's nice and cool in here," I said. "There's no water to drown in."

"Will you get out, you foolish cat?" the dog demanded.

The dog barked and barked, but I ignored him, and he lay down in front of the machine. Soon we were both asleep.

Suddenly I heard a loud, terrible growling. What was that? I gave my head a little shake and realized the growling was coming from my dog. What was wrong now?

When I looked out of the machine, I saw one of the young men lean over. He threw some towels into the machine, and then he opened a little door in the front of the machine, and soap powder sifted down, making me sneeze. Then he slammed the door to the machine. I saw him lean forward again and heard the dial on top of the machine begin to twist.

Suddenly my dog leaped up and grabbed the man's arm with his teeth.

"Get down! Bad dog!" the young man shouted. He shook himself loose from Sam.

But when he again leaned over and tried to turn the dial, Sam again leaped and grabbed him by the arm. This time the young man shrieked in pain. Within minutes, another young man came running down the steps.

"The dog's gone crazy!" the first one shouted. "He bit me! He won't let me near the washing machine!"

The second young man ran upstairs and came down with a rolled-up newspaper. He hit Sam on the head with it—hard. Then the first young man reached for the washing machine dial. Sam jumped up and bit down on his arm. He dragged him from the machine and barked as loud as he could. He stood, his nose pointing at the machine, one paw raised and tucked under.

Inside the machine, I started to scream. No one was going to hurt my dog!

"What was that?" asked the first young man.

"I think it came from the machine," said the second.

I screamed again. I screamed until my throat hurt and my ears bubbled.

"It *is* coming from the machine," said the second young man. "Open the door!"

They opened the door, and I leaped out, hissing and spitting. I landed on the first man's chest and sank my nails into his shirt. I would teach him to hurt my dog!

"Get this cat away from me!" he said, but the second man simply stood there.

"We almost drowned him," the second one said. "If we'd turned on the machine, it would have been the end of him. That's why the dog went for you."

I let go and dropped to the floor. I ran over to my dog, my fur standing on end, my ears flattened against my head.

The two of them turned and looked at the two of us.

"Make sure you keep that door locked," said the second man, and the first one said he would.

"Look at that cat," said the first man. "All full of soap powder."

"He's lucky to be alive," said the second one.

"I don't know about that dog," said the first man. "He's vicious. I'm putting him out in the yard for a few days."

For the next few days, Sam was locked out in the yard. I climbed up onto the sofa and watched him through the window. He lay still on the back porch, his head on his crossed paws. He rarely looked at me.

When he came back, I apologized and apologized. I said never again would I go into a machine. Never again would I disobey him.

"You say that now," said Sam.

"I mean it!" I cried.

"You should," Sam said. "You lost one of your nine lives in that machine."

"Well," I said grumpily, because I was tired of being scolded, "I have already been punished. When I cleaned myself, I had to lick away the soapsuds. They gave me a terrible stomach ache."

"Good," said Sam.

"And anyway," I said defiantly, "I wouldn't have drowned. I would have swum very fast."

"You would have been pulled down by heavy wet towels and you would have drowned," said Sam. "You know that as well as I do."

I licked my paw, and looked at him from under lowered lids.

"Is what I say true, or isn't it?" Sam asked me.

"I suppose it is," I said.

"Is it or isn't it?" Sam demanded.

"It is," I said.

"You won't do it again?"

"No," I said. "I told you."

"Good," said Sam.

"I'm sorry they put you out there where it was so hot," I said.

"Hot and full of fleas," said Sam.

"It was my fault," I said.

My dog didn't answer me.

"Warm won't like the fleas, will she?" I asked.

"She won't," Sam said. "She won't like to hear I bit that man either."

Now when they put Sam out in the yard, they left him there for a long time. While he was on the porch, I stayed on the couch and watched him, trying to keep him company. It was the least I could do.

If this was summer, I thought, I didn't like it.

"You are a good dog," I told Sam again and again. "They are bad men for punishing you. I am a bad cat. I shouldn't have gone in that machine."

"Everyone makes mistakes," said Sam. He licked me from head to tail. I was wet and cool.

"You are *my* dog," I said, purring happily.

"You are *my* cat," he said.

And then one day a cool breeze blew in the window, and I sighed to feel it, a tiny sound of contentment, because all day it had been so hot. Just then, the front doorbell rang, and one of the men opened the door, and whose voice did I hear? It was Warm's! And I jumped down from the window and ran into the hall to greet her, as I always did, but when she caught sight of me, she cried out in alarm.

"Oh, look at poor Foudini!" she said, and she swept me up in her arms. "Oh, look how fat he has gotten, and how dirty!" she said, and meanwhile my dog was leaping up against her so that she had to stand against the wall, or he would have knocked her down. He had his front paws pressed against her chest, and he was licking her face, and his tail beat back and forth, stirring the warm air into a wind.

Then Pest came through the door, and the dog threw himself at him, and Warm carried me to the couch and set me on her lap and began combing me with her fingers and singing my Foudini song to me, and her fingers felt for my collar, and she said, "Why is this collar so tight?" and she loosened it, and she sang, "You are my Foudini, my only Dini, / You make me happy when skies are gray, / If you only knew, Fou, how much I love you, / Please don't take my Foudini away," and I knew all was again right with the world, and it was, because Pest must have chased the three men out, and I thought, Good, now we will never see them again. Now we will never again hear the horrible sounds they made as they sawed up whatever they were sawing on the front porch. I would protect Warm and everyone else in the house as long as I lived—even Pest.

The next day a chill wind began to blow in through the windows, and in no time at all, I was a clean cat, and in no time at all, I was given back my plates of steaming meat. I ran through the rooms chasing my dog, and running from him when he chased me, and soon it was winter again, and I was once more perfectly happy. Naturally I forgot that the dog said Warm and Pest would leave every year when the weather grew warm. I said to myself, It may never grow warm again. After all, look at how cold it is now. Look at the snow swirling outside the window.

I was careful of Warm and watched her narrowly, and when she put evil-smelling pills into her hand and was about to put them in her mouth, I jumped at her and batted the pills from her hand. She was annoyed with me and searched the floor until she found them, and in spite of all my efforts, she swallowed them. But nothing happened to her, as far as I could see.

"These are good things," she said to me. And I knew she was angry, so I pretended to chase one of the pills about the kitchen floor.

"All right, keep that one," Warm said. "But don't eat it."

I had no intention of eating it.

The dog was so happy to see them that he became quite talkative and told me the story of how he had first come to live in the city house, and when he came, he said, he was not at all used to Warm and Pest, and he missed his mother and the other puppies who all chewed on one another and were not scolded, and regardless of how often he was coaxed, he would not climb up onto the bed with Warm and Pest. Soon he grew quite big, and when he stood up, he could place his paws on Warm's shoulders.

"They came to the house where I lived with my mother and picked me from all the others," the dog said, "because I had such big feet. They wanted a dog who would sit in the window seat and look over the street and frighten everyone off, and puppies with big feet grow up to be big dogs, just as I did.

"And in time, I was happy with them. You mustn't think I was unhappy. But I refused to climb on the bed, because one day I was lying on the bed and absentmind-edly began chewing on the footboard, and Pest hit me with a rolled-up newspaper. I decided the bed was a dangerous place.

"But then one night there was a terrible thunder-storm, and lightning flashed through the room, turning everything silver and gray, and I lay on the floor shivering and afraid. You know I am terrified of thunder and lightning. There was a particularly enormous clap of thunder, and I was so frightened that I jumped up onto the bed. Do you know what happened? I was so big that there was no room for anyone, and Warm fell off her side of the bed, and Pest fell off his side. They climbed back onto the bed and held on to my collar so they would not fall off again, and they went back to sleep, and I went to sleep, and I realized that this was how we should sleep, all in a heap, as I had done when I was a very young dog, and in the morning, we were inseparable, just as you see us now, and I learned to sleep at the foot of the bed so that Warm and Pest would have enough room, even though I was there. Even so, Warm has to sleep with her legs drawn up, because I sleep on her side of the bed. Pest is tall, and he pokes at me with his feet.

"That is how I came here, and how I learned to sleep on the bed."

"I have large feet," I said. "Will I grow to be a large cat?"

"You are already a large cat," said the dog. "And your feet are not so very large. They are large enough for *you*, which is what matters."

"I think they are quite large," I said, lifting my paw and looking at it.

"I am sure they would have picked you out of a pile of kittens," said the dog.

"Did you know there were other cats here before us?" I ask her, and she says, "Oh? Where did they go?" I say, "Oh, off to another house." Grace the Cat is a little and very young cat. She does not want to know about cats who stop moving and cannot be awakened, even by dishes of steaming food.

And today, what a commotion! Snow began falling during the night, and when the light returned, fat snowflakes were swirling outside all the windows, and Grace the Cat had never seen this before. She sat in the window and cried to the snowflakes, and stood up against the glass and tried to catch them as they hit the panes, and I understood that she thought the snowflakes were tiny white birds, and she wanted to catch them and eat them. All day, she has been crying out to the snowflakes and twitching her tail and observing how a snowflake hits the window and then disappears, and in its place leaves drops of water that run down the glass, and then she cries with disappointment and confusion. She is still a very young cat.

Did I ever cry out to snowflakes, trying to persuade them into my mouth? I cannot believe I ever did such a thing, but if Grace is doing that now, probably I myself was once as foolish.

When Warm and Pest returned, bringing their gray boxes full of strange smells that even my dog could not identify, we were so overjoyed that we could barely contain ourselves. In our exuberance, we began thinking up new tricks.

"I want those dog biscuits," the dog said, looking sadly at the box on top of the refrigerator. "But I am not quite tall enough. I tried climbing up on a chair, but I was too big and fell off."

"Warm says you eat too many," I said.

The dog looked longingly up at his dog biscuits.

Warm would not like it if I knocked the box down. But Warm was not here. She had gone out, gotten in the car, and driven off.

I was again a slender cat, so I jumped up on a chair, and from the chair to the top of the refrigerator, and with my head, I began pushing the box of biscuits forward. The dog whined in expectation. I stopped. Another push and the box would be on the floor. The dog whined loudly. He was, after all, my dog. He knew when he was hungry. Warm did not always know, and sometimes we were very hungry when she finally decided to feed us. I pushed the box farther, and it toppled to the floor.

The dog picked up one paw and placed it on the box, and with his great teeth, he ripped the box open. In a short time, he had eaten all the biscuits. He lay on the floor and burped with satisfaction.

"Oh, this is very bad," Warm said when she came back. "How did you get that box?" She looked at the top of the refrigerator where the box had been, and then down at the floor, at the wet, crumpled box. "You didn't help him, did you?" she asked me. I licked my paw and then began washing my tail. "Of course you didn't," she said.

I purred happily on the floor.

But this gave me an idea. I was always hungry in the morning, and often when I opened my eyes, Warm was still happily asleep. No matter how loudly I cried, she refused to stir from her bed. I took to climbing up on the high headboard and leaping from it onto the bed.

In the beginning, this worked well. The sudden thump I made when I landed on Warm's chest woke her quite nicely, and then she would get up, go down to the kitchen, and fill up my empty plate. But now she managed to sleep through my leaps. And when I put out my claws and began to pet her on the cheek, she pulled the blankets up over her head and slept on.

I must try more drastic measures, I thought. But what? This was quite a challenge. Warm was as determined to sleep as I was to get her up when I was ready to eat.

I thought, I will jump onto the chest of drawers and throw things from it to the floor.

I threw down Warm's brush, but still she did not stir. I threw down a book, and she slept on. I could see I was going to be a hungry cat until late in the morning. At night, I would get up on Warm's bed and cry when she went by, meaning to say, *It is time for you to come to bed.* Some nights she listened to me, but other nights she defied me and stayed up even later than Pest, typing on her uninteresting machine. It was because of that machine that she slept so late and refused to get up and feed me.

I saw the glass bottle on the bureau. Once before I had knocked such a thing down, and the most interesting thing happened. The bottle hit the floor and splintered into pieces. I thought, Now I will push this bottle onto the floor and make it turn into a not-bottle, and then she will be sorry. I began moving the bottle slowly toward the rim of the bureau. Aha! The woman was picking her head up from the pillow. I pushed the bottle forward, and Warm sat up in bed. And just as I was about to topple the bottle over the edge, Warm sprang up, seized the bottle, and followed me out onto the landing and down into the kitchen, where she opened a can of my food and put it on a plate.

"Bad cat," she said, and went back up the steps and closed the bedroom door. I listened at the door. I heard the bed creak. She had gone back to bed. Without me! Had I outsmarted myself? Would she now lock me out of the room at night?

But that night, she called to me and patted the empty space next to her, and I jumped into the bed and waited for her to cover me up and put her arm over me.

"What a wonderful purr," she said. "Better than a sleeping pill. You put me to sleep. Good cat, nice cat."

Oh, yes, good cat, nice cat, I thought, and in the

morning, hungry cat, but I know how to take care of that. She has several bottles on her chest of drawers. I will start with the small one, and if that doesn't get her up, I will go on to the next one and the next one.

The following morning, I was up on the chest of drawers, entirely satisfied with myself, pushing the small bottle to the edge, when Warm jumped up. She followed me out the door. I had my tail in the air, and my mouth was watering, when I heard the door slam behind me. Foiled!

I went down to the kitchen, and the dog obligingly ripped open my bag of dried food. I had to make do with that. How was I going to entice the woman out of her room and down into the kitchen? That was the trouble with humans, I found—and still find. They learn so fast.

Of course, I was a very young cat when I did these wicked things. These days I know better. When I see Grace beginning to knock things from the chest of drawers, I hiss at her, slap her bottom, and chase her down onto the floor.

But you must not go too far. You must not become too well behaved. Human beings, even Warm, can become forgetful and begin to take you for granted. Humans like Warm wander down into the kitchen, stare out the window—but they are not looking for anything, not even a squirrel or a bird, not even another cat—they stare up at the wall and look at the bright bracelets on their arms and shake their heads; they sit down in chairs and pick up yesterday's magazines, and all the time, there you are, standing on the floor, waiting for them to open a can of your tinned mice. Finally, they go to the drawer and take out a spoon and advance, you hope, upon your store of food. At the last instant, they stop and resume their staring out the uneventful window. Even if you rub up against their legs, or stand up and place your paws upon their knees, they continue to hold a spoon and stare—as if they have been turned into trees.

I will not put up with this. At some point you have to draw the line. And so I encourage Grace to cry at the top of her lungs when she is hungry, and I cry along with her because I have a louder and more raspy voice and am more likely to get the attention of the humans around me.

But it is surprising how loudly we can cry outside Warm's bedroom door, and still she does not hear us.

"Cry as loud as you can," I told Grace, and I opened my own mouth and made a dreadful noise.

I watched Grace, who opened her mouth wide and cried with all her might, but all the same, only a tiny sound flew from her throat.

"Is that the best you can do?" I asked her, disgusted. "What a noise you make if anyone steps on your tail!"

"I cry my everyday cry at all times," Grace said indignantly, when in fact she shrieks so loudly that anyone who had the misfortune to step on her tail jumps in the air and clutches at his chest, startled half out of his wits.

"It is a good thing for you," I told her, "that I am always hungry and always vigilant, or you would starve to death. If I were not here to watch you, you would throw down every bottle in the house, Warm would lock you in the basement, and you would not eat until morning, and the light would shine through you as it does through that window there."

Grace bobbed her head while licking her paw and watched me out of the corner of her eye. She does not like to be scolded, and so I was not surprised when, a few minutes later, I was lying peacefully on the living room rug and Grace leaped upon me, grabbing me by the neck and aiming the paws of her back legs at my head.

"Briiiiip," I said, meaning *Let go of me this instant.* But Grace paid no attention. Instead, she jumped up onto the couch and launched herself at me again, this time landing on my full stomach. "Briiiiip," I said, which also means *Don't sit on me, don't attack me, leave me in peace.* And I turned over, my stomach up in the air. You would have thought this would be warning enough. But Grace promptly jumped upon my stomach, *bounced* upon it, and then ran through the rooms making all her warlike sounds.

I will have no peace now, I thought.

I was right, because Grace stole back into the room,

seized me by the neck, and began pulling on my fur until I thought I would be yanked straight out of my cat suit. Naturally I began to scream. Warm rushed in.

"Oh, it is only you two fighting again," Warm said, and she sat down in a chair and watched us. I screamed again, half in indignation, half in fear, because Grace had torn loose a part of me and was pulling whatever it was over my ears.

"Oh, Grace!" said Warm. "You've taken off his collar! Don't do that! That's a bad cat!"

Now she spoke up, after little Grace had half throttled me!

But what was that, lying on the floor? I got up and inspected it. It smelled like me. It looked like my collar. But if it was my collar, something I had worn from my first day in the house, what was it doing on the floor? And what did I think of this new feeling, this without-collarness? When I turned my head from side to side, something was missing—the feel of that collar. I scratched behind my ear. My claws did not strike the collar. What would happen now? It must be important for a cat to wear a collar, or why would Warm always insist we wear one?

Perhaps my head might fall off.

"Come look at this," Warm called out. "Grace took off Foudini's collar, and now they're both sitting here staring at me."

"They are idiots," said Pest, as he came into the room.

"I think she did it deliberately," Warm said.

But she did not do it deliberately! Grace had been trying to strangle me, and she removed the collar accidentally. Or so I thought, until later that night when Grace began rolling frantically about the floor, crying in her little voice, which was still the voice of a kitten, and when she stopped, her plaid collar was not around her neck, but was lying on the floor just as mine had been.

We both inspected Grace's collar. We wondered what would happen to us now that we had no collars around our neck.

Nothing happened. Warm picked up the collars, and when I was sitting in her lap, she refastened the collar around my neck, and a few days later, she managed to do the same to a squirming Grace.

"You see?" I said. "Once the humans make up their minds, there's no changing them. Give up on these collars."

Grace slit her eyes at me and went off into the kitchen, where I knew she would be chewing on the leaves of Warm's one remaining houseplant. I waited for Warm to shout, "Bad cat!" It did not take her long.

When I went into the kitchen, there were little holes in most of the leaves. Grace hadn't even bothered to chew on the leaves she had torn from the plant, so I chewed them up and ate them. These green leaves were excellent for removing fur balls, as I well knew. When I coughed up a fur ball, Grace, who always panicked at the coughing, choking sounds I made, would be sorry she had attacked me and had torn away my collar.

This, naturally, was what happened, and when I was finished coughing and choking, Grace had a worried look. Now she wanted once again to be in my good graces. She lay down in front of me and began licking me between the eyes. I ignored her. She pretended to swat at my ear. I put my paw out, pushed hard on her forehead between her ears, and held her off. I wouldn't look at her. Finally, she lay down next to me, sighed deeply, and went to sleep.

I got up and jumped onto the couch. If that cat would not take my advice, if she would sulk and become vengeful whenever I criticized her, she could sleep by herself on the floor.

I fell asleep on the couch and was sleeping peacefully when a horrible scream woke me. It was Warm screaming! I jumped down from the couch and ran upstairs to the bedroom. Warm saw me and pointed to the bed and screamed again and again.

I jumped up onto the bed. Perhaps a snake had gotten in from the garden. I would kill the snake and protect Warm.

But there was no snake. There was a bloody mouse, its head half chewed away. The mouse had been placed carefully on Warm's pillow. So that was why Warm was screaming.

I picked up the mouse and jumped down from the bed. I intended to hide the mouse behind a cabinet or under a carpet.

"How could you put it there, you bad cat!" Warm shouted at me. "Go away! Take that mouse away!"

Grace appeared in the doorway.

"Look what he did!" Warm said to Grace.

Grace rubbed up against Warm's legs as if to comfort her. Warm bent down and picked her up. I was to be blamed for Grace's doings!

"You bad cat!" I growled at Grace.

"Don't you growl at her, you bloody-mouthed thing!" said Warm. She petted Grace. "Out of the room!" she said to me.

I left, carrying the dead mouse.

How unfair the world can be! If I was to be blamed, I should have had the pleasure of chewing up the mouse. I particularly liked crunching its head. But this mouse was stiff and stale, and its smell was not pleasant. I went downstairs and hid the mouse behind the dining room sideboard.

Later, Grace came over to me and tried to lick my head.

"I don't want to have anything to do with you," I said. "You were happy I was blamed."

"Someone had to be blamed," Grace said.

I ignored her. Even when she jumped on me, I didn't move.

Grace, however, could never bear to be spurned for long, and she began throwing her toy mouse into the air, chasing after it, and bringing it back to me, dropping it right under my nose.

Naturally, I forgave her.

Not long after Grace removed our collars and displayed her bloody mouse on the big bed, she discovered the hall mirror, as sooner or later we all do. Ordinarily, I would not have seen this happen, because I do not usually follow that annoying creature about the house, but Grace, who believed she was seeing another cat in the mirror, immediately set up a dreadful howl, and I came flying down the steps to see what the trouble was.

Grace had crept up to the mirror until her nose was almost pressed against the nose of the cat she saw in the glass. She reached out one paw to touch the cat, but when her paw touched the mirror, she withdrew it and again stared into the mirror.

"There is a cat in there," Grace said softly, "but it has no smell and no voice. What kind of cat can it be?"

"It is not a real cat," I said, coming up behind Grace. "It is a ghost cat. They live in mirrors. Whenever you go near a mirror, one of them comes to see you, and whatever you do, that is what the ghost cat will do. Try. Do something."

Grace rolled on her back and looked over her shoulder at the mirror. There was the ghost cat, lying on its back, looking at her.

"You see?" I told her.

"Does this ghost cat catch ghost mice?" she asked me. She was forever hopeful, that cat.

"If you are catching mice in front of the mirror, then the ghost cat will catch one, too."

"And can I eat her mouse?"

"It is not a real mouse," I said.

"You think you know everything," Grace said, lying down in front of the mirror. "I believe I will just stay here. What a beautiful cat it is, that cat. I wish I could go in there and play with that new cat."

I sighed, and went off to find Warm. She was sitting in a living room chair, watching ghost people move about in a large black box. "Jump up," she said to me, patting her lap. Whenever the ghost people moved about in the black box, Warm stayed in her chair for quite some time watching them. I thought it was well worth my while to jump up and settle myself against her chest and tilt my head up so that I could stare into her eyes when she petted me and looked down at me. Then we would stare into one another's eyes, and whenever I did, I would see two tiny cats, one in each of her eyes. It seemed to me that these cats were not ghost cats, but real ones who had my own smell. Often I would reach out with one paw, trying to touch these cats, but then Warm would blink her eyes and turn her head away from me, and so I knew she did not want me to touch those cats because they were so small and I might harm them.

Perhaps, I thought, this is how cats came to be invented. Human beings thought them up, and somehow they began to exist in the world. If that were so, there must be many cats who looked like me—I had seen many ghost cats who looked like me in the hall mirror—because the cats in Warm's eyes looked exactly like me. But it was possible that cats were invented even before people, and human beings began to appear in *their* eyes, and one day the humans stepped out somehow and began to walk about the earth.

Who came first, the humans or the cats? I decided the cats must have come first, because they ran so much faster and so could better escape their enemies, and they could climb trees in a few seconds and would be safe from whatever hunted them on the ground. Yes, the cats came first, and eventually, the humans became smarter and learned how to build houses, and then nothing could get at them, even though they could not run quickly or leap into trees. Why had this not been plain to me from the beginning?

I reached up, again trying to touch one of Warm's

eyes, but she blinked and once more turned her head from me. I looked into her eyes, watching the little cats until I fell asleep.

Meanwhile, Grace had opened a cabinet and climbed in, looking for our special cat candies. She was a clever cat, that Grace. She could open almost anything. She could not open the boxes into which we were packed when Warm and Pest took us to Mouse House, but then she liked going to Mouse House, and so she would not try.

Grace came into the room and lay down with a thump. "What a boring cat is that ghost cat," she said. "She spends hours licking her stupid paws," she said as she licked her own paw.

You think, especially if you are a cat, that everything will forever be as it is when you look about you.

I thought, of course, that I would always have my dog. He would never run away, not for good, although he often waited at the door and ran past Warm and out the gate when he saw it was unfastened, and then Warm would run out after him. At times, she would have to chase him for blocks before she caught up with him. One morning, someone left the gate open, and naturally the dog ran through it, and Warm, still in her sleeping coat, flew out after him, but she was soon back with him, angry and scolding.

When we were at Mouse House, he would sometimes disappear for hours. When he came back, he smelled of wonderful, strange animals. Once he ran back onto the porch with a lamb chop in his mouth, and lay down eating it happily, and once Warm told Pest, "He stole six steaks from a barbecue, and the man said he wanted to shoot him, and I said, 'I'll replace the steaks. You don't have to shoot the dog.' "

Shoot the dog!

"We will have to be more careful," said Pest.

"Oh, yes," said Warm.

"Especially during hunting season," said Pest. "He's so big someone might mistake him for a deer."

"I'll tie a red scarf around his neck," Warm said.

Shoot the dog! Could someone shoot my dog? Could someone come to the window of my house and shoot me?

"You should stay in the house with me," I told the dog.

"No one is going to shoot me," he said. He got up and went to the window, and as he walked across the room, I saw that he had begun to limp. I thought, When he lies down, I will check his paws. I will see if he has anything stuck in them.

But he did not have anything stuck in them, and after a short time, he stopped limping. We no longer heard the popping sounds, which Warm said was a gun going off, and so I stopped worrying.

But my dog began limping more and more, and often he cried out when he stood up. I did not like this, and I began to follow the dog about, licking him frequently between the ears, and kept on licking him until he began to growl. I licked his paws and caught the bits of fur that grew beneath the pads of his feet in my mouth, but I found nothing, and I annoyed the dog, who would turn to me, place his long nose under my stomach, lift me into the air, and then put me down.

All this happened before the arrival of Grace the Cat, who does not understand why, these days, when I hear a great, thundering bark, I pick up my head and listen carefully, and sometimes even go to the window, thinking, Is it my dog? Is that my dog locked out of the house?

Grace thinks I am frightened of the barking dog and curls herself up in a ball, twitches her tail as she looks at me, and says, "How silly you are to worry! That dog cannot get in here and hurt us."

One day my dog could not get up, but could only drag himself across the floor by his front paws, and I was busy carrying pieces of our meat from our dish to the living room, where he was lying still and whining. Just then, Warm came in.

"What is the matter with you?" she asked the dog, who struggled to get up and walk over to her. But he could not make his back legs obey him, and he again collapsed on the floor. He dragged himself to her. When

Warm saw this, she stood up and came to the dog and sat down on the floor next to him. The dog put his head in her lap, and she petted him for a long time, and then she called out to Pest, who came running down the steps.

"I'll start the car," Pest said, and he took my dog's collar and leash down from the wall. Ordinarily, when I saw this, I would immediately flee into the cellar and hide in the rafters so that they would have to come down and plead with me, and at last they would have to take a broom and poke it into my hiding places until I decided to come out. This time I knew they weren't about to pack me, and I thought, I will go with the dog because he is unhappy, and if he is unhappy, I should go with him and lick him between the ears. I marched bravely over to my blue box and waited for one of them to seize me and pack me. No one was interested! No one bent down to grab me and stuff me as quickly as possible into my box.

What is going on here? I asked myself. This is not the normal way of the world.

I watched while Pest fastened the leash hook to the dog's collar. The dog began to whine excitedly, and I thought, Surely he will get up now. Surely now he understands they are going to take him for a ride in that car he loves so much. And still he could not make himself stand up. When Pest saw this, he picked up the dog, and from the windowsill I watched as he was carried out to the car and put in the backseat. Warm climbed in next to the dog, and Pest drove off.

Now I began to worry. What does it mean when someone goes away in a car? They may only be going to Mouse House, I thought, but they had left me alone in the city house, and I knew they would not do that if they were going far away. Were they taking the dog far away? Would they leave him somewhere—as my mother had left me in the warm basement when she went out to hunt for food and never came back? And if they did leave him far from the house, how could he find his way back to us? How could he travel over his Map of Smells if he could not make his back legs listen to him?

I waited at the window and watched for the dog. I saw two birds sitting on the branch of a tree. I saw one squirrel chase another over the roof of the garage. The wind blew hard and rustled the dry leaves that still clung to the trees. Someone rang the bell, and I heard mail hit the porch floor, but the dog was not there, and so he did not bark. I asked myself, What will I do without my dog? He spends the days and nights with me. When Warm and Pest are not here, he sleeps next to me and he plays with me. We chase each other through the house. Once when I was climbing a curtain and caught my claw, he climbed up on the couch and got me by the collar and pulled me loose.

I tried to remember: Had Warm said "Back soon" as she left? Whenever she said "Back soon," she was not gone for long. When she and Pest left with their big gray boxes, she did not say "Back soon." I didn't think she had said "Back soon" when she left with the dog.

I waited and waited, and eventually I grew discouraged and began to think again about my mother, who went out to hunt and never returned. I went upstairs and lay down in front of the hall mirror and looked at the ghost cat who stared back at me.

"Where is my dog?" I asked the ghost cat, but the ghost cat looked sadly at me and said, "Where is *my* dog?"

I curled myself into a tight ball and went to sleep, and when I slept, I dreamed of wolves leaping against a tree into which I had climbed, but just as I began to fear them, all the wolves began to cry piteously, and all of them fell onto the ground and could not get up.

"Get up! Get up!" I cried to the wolves, who looked at me with sad eyes and cried even louder, until I began to climb down the tree trunk toward them. I will hit them on the nose, I thought. I will hit them hard with my claws out, and then they will get up. They will see that they can walk if they want to walk!

But when I reached the first wolf and hit him on the nose, he did not get up. He looked at me and cried louder.

"I will put on your collar and take you in the car," I told him, but he didn't understand me, and only growled and cried.

Just then, I heard the slam of a car door, and I flew downstairs. Where was my dog?

He wasn't there!

"He'll be back soon," said Warm, and she picked me up and held me close to her.

"I don't know how you can pick him up," said Pest. "He is so heavy."

She didn't answer him. She nuzzled my fur. She buried her face in my side. And I smelled the unmistakable smell—*hospital!* She smelled of the hospital! So that was where she had taken the dog! But then why hadn't she brought him back? He wasn't used to staying there without me. When we both went to the hospital, the doctor put us both in one wire box because, if we were separated, we would cry one to the other and cause an uproar among the other animals.

"He will be fine," said Warm, her nose buried in my fur.

"I hope so," Pest said gloomily.

He will escape, I thought. He will pick the lock of his wire box, or he will pull the door open; he is such a strong dog and such a smart dog. In the middle of the night, I will hear his scratching at the door, and I will shriek and scream until they wake up and let him in. I refused to go to sleep, but kept my ears pointed up toward the ceiling, listening for him.

When the light came back, I was still on the bed next to Warm, and when I got up and looked at the foot of the bed, the dog was still not there, and later, when they put my dish of food before me, I could not eat. I was accustomed to the dog's head next to mine. I was accustomed to pushing his head away from my side of the plate and his pushing me away from his portion of the meat.

A whole plate to myself! What could be more dreadful?

So we change, without even knowing we are changing.

The light came and went and came and went, and still there was no sign of the dog. Still he did not open his wire cage and follow home his Map of Smells.

Well, he is not coming, I thought. There is nothing I can do about it. I lay down on the living room couch and turned my back to the world. When Warm saw this, she picked me up, settled me on her lap, and petted me for a long time. She got up and brought back a ball on a string and dangled it in front of me, hoping I would swat at it, but I had no interest in strings. I wanted her to bring back the dog. She herself had helped carry him off.

"You have to eat," she said that night, "or we will have to take you to the hospital, too." She dipped her finger into a glass of water and brushed my nose with the liquid, and I automatically licked my nose. She kept this up until I had a good drink. Then I felt better, although I refused to eat or to run through the house.

And the next day the sun came up, and still there was no dog.

I was asleep in the rafters thinking I would stay there forever and never come down, asking myself what kind of world was it when everyone vanished, when people and dogs and mothers walked through doors and never walked back in. What kind of animals were on the other side of the door who swallowed up dogs whole? What kind of world was it when your legs stopped working, and you could no longer cross a room? It was no kind of world at all! It was not a world I wanted to live in! And just as I was thinking this, I heard the dog's loud bark. My dog was back!

I rushed upstairs. I threw myself upon the dog. I stood up and held on to the dog's neck with my paws. I leaped around him and grabbed on to his tail, biting down with joy, and so I did not immediately notice that the dog did not chase after me, but in a few minutes, I saw it. The dog still could not walk.

Now Pest carried the dog into the living room, and Warm put a little bed in front of the couch. On top of that she put blankets, and I soon understood that she meant to sleep downstairs with the dog. Well, then, I thought, I will sleep here as well. I will find out what happened to my dog, and I will watch in the night while everyone sleeps.

"In the hospital, they tried to fix me, but my legs will not work," said the dog.

I said, "Don't worry. They will work soon." Then I pressed my head close to the dog's, so that I could see what he had seen, and I found myself looking out through the doctor's wire cages. A doctor was coming toward me with the sharp, shining thing that bit into my side like a flea. Then the doctor went away, and I was again alone in my cage. Somewhere on the other side of the room, a lonely cat wailed and licked at its bloody stomach.

"Next time I will go with you," I told the dog.

"Go to sleep," the dog said to me.

The next morning, Warm fed us, and Pest carried the dog out into the backyard, and that night, Warm again slept on the bed in the living room.

Well, this is what our lives will be like now, I thought. Warm will sleep down here, and the dog will be carried in and out, and there will be no more chases through the house. I will come in here and climb up on the dog's back and lie there and lick at his fur.

But that day, when Warm went upstairs to type on her machine, the dog began to cry and struggle to his feet, and the next thing I knew, he was walking—not well, not at all well, he kept falling down, but he was walking. He was using all four legs. And while I watched him, he went to the stairs and began trying to climb them.

"Get off those steps!" I told him. "You will fall down and that will make everything worse!"

"A dog has one job," he said, "and that is to stay with his people."

"I am your people!" I said, and he said yes, I was also his people, but he was climbing up the steps, and nothing was going to stop him, and then he lost his balance and slid down and landed on top of me.

I began to howl.

Warm rushed to the top of the steps, leaned over the railing, and looked down. "What is that dog doing?" she said.

"You see!" I told the dog. "You see! She doesn't want you on the steps! Get down!"

But the dog tried again, and this time he was halfway up before he lost his balance, and when he did, he did not fall all the way down. Warm saw what he was doing and came downstairs. She grabbed hold of the dog's collar and helped pull him along as he scrabbled up the steps, until finally he had reached the second floor.

"What a stubborn dog you are," Warm said admiringly, and she went downstairs and brought him a dog biscuit. "Foudini, did you ever see anything like this?" she asked me. Naturally, I hadn't, and I hoped never to see anything like it again. And soon the dog climbed up to the third floor, and shortly after that, he was climbing up and down, almost as if nothing had ever happened.

But I noticed that now he limped almost all the time, and there were days when he lay in one place and cried softly to himself, and then no matter how I licked him or danced about, threatening to hit him on the nose, he would not move, and on those days, I would do my hunting and prowling, and when I was finished, I would come back and lie next to him, or on him, holding on to his collar with my front paws so that I did not slide off.

"And did he live forever?" Grace the Cat asks me, and I wonder again what she finds to think about that is so important, because clearly she does not think about what I have to tell her.

"Well, he is not here now," I say.

"Probably he is living in the woods near Mouse House," she says.

"Probably," I say.

"Why does Warm keep saying she wants another dog?" she wants to know. "*I* don't want a dog. I am more than enough for myself!"

"You are forgetting me, aren't you?" I ask her. "It is because of me that you were brought here in the first place."

"Exactly what I meant," she says, lazily stretching herself into a crescent shape. "I am enough for everyone."

"Don't forget me!" I complain.

"Naturally not," she says, not bothering to look at me. She is still a young cat.

I see that I have neglected to talk about the child, and how surprising that is, when once he was so important to us and we were so important to him. I well remember the day when Warm and Pest brought home an evil-smelling creature wrapped in a blanket, and Warm showed the dog the little waving thing and said, "This is a puppy child," and the child began to howl. I fled from the room, followed by the panic-stricken dog.

But we were soon back, watching Warm hold the child and feed it milk from a bottle, just as she had fed me my medicine when she first brought me home. She sprinkled the child with white powder, just as she had sprinkled me, so I knew the child had fleas, but soon the fleas would be gone.

"The child doesn't have fleas; don't be silly," said the dog. "The child has no fur."

There is no point in arguing with dogs, or so I have always found. They will simply grow angry and bite down harder than you would like.

The child must have had many fleas—that was plain to see—because the woman powdered him several times a day. I disliked this because the white powdery cloud always made me sneeze, and so I learned to leave the room before she began to shake the powder upon him.

There was a tall bookshelf in the child's room, and I took to sleeping on the shelf above his bassinet, and when he cried, I would jump down, look for Warm, and call out until she asked me what I wanted. She soon learned I wanted her to follow me back to the child's room. When she saw the child was crying, she would pick him up, put him on a table, clean him and powder him, and replace him in his bassinet and go downstairs to find a bottle of milk for him.

I did not sit in Warm's lap as often as I used to, but I foresaw that this small creature would one day have a lap of his own, and then I could sit on him. He was already creeping about the floor on all fours as if he were a cat or a dog, not a human. No wonder she calls him a puppy child, I thought.

"When she brought *you* home," the dog said to me, "she called *you* a puppy cat. 'Be nice to the puppy cat' is what she said."

" 'Puppy cat'?"

"She knows I like puppies," the dog said, looking away. He was embarrassed.

"And did you think I was a puppy?" I asked him.

"You lived with me and you were mine. You *might* have been part puppy," he said.

The dog, meanwhile, had taken it upon himself to keep the small thing from destroying itself, which it often seemed intent on doing.

The small one would creep out of its room and onto the landing, and from the landing, it would crawl off in the direction of the stairs. If I saw this, I would set up quite a howl, and the dog would come from whatever room he was in. Then he would stand over the small thing, and with his left paw he would push back the little thing's left shoulder, and with his right paw he would push back the little one's right shoulder, and then he would back up and do this again and again, until the little creature was safely back in his room. Once he was where he ought to be, the dog would lie down across the threshold. He was so large that the little one could not climb over him.

"What excellent baby-sitters you are!" Warm said in those days, and we were very pleased. We must have done our job quite well, because soon the little one stood up on his hind legs and began walking through the house, crashing into furniture and tripping over us on his way to the stairs. Then the dog would sink his teeth into the child's pajama bottoms and pull him back, and if the child tried to approach the stairs again, the dog would begin to bark, and eventually the child learned not to defy him. When the dog barked, the little one would turn around and go back to his room.

The dog and the child had now become great friends, but I was not so sure about this child. He was not, according to me, coming along well. He would shriek at the sight of me, such a loud sound and so high pitched that my ears would hurt for a long time afterward. He would grab my tail and chew on it. He pulled my fur. He hit me on the head with a cloth monkey he wielded by the tail.

The dog did not seem to mind any of this, but the dog was much larger than I was, and taller, and if the child annoyed him, he would gently topple him to the floor, put a paw over him, and the child could not move.

"You will see," said the dog. "He will grow into a person just like Warm and Pest."

"He is rude and smelly and he will do nothing of the kind," I said.

"You'll see," said the dog, and he was right.

But when the child grew larger and began to look like Warm and Pest, I was disappointed. Now he was only another human being. He was no longer *ours*. He no longer crawled about the floor, only a little taller than me, but not as tall as the dog.

Time passed, and the child grew and grew, and soon he began to feed us himself. Before we knew it, he began to leave early every morning, and then the dog and I were once more in a quiet house waiting for Warm and Pest to return from their many hunting expeditions.

"I hope he will be home soon so he will throw my green frog," the dog said.

"I hope he will come home and wiggle my string for me," I said.

"Don't you like my green frog?" the dog asked me. "It is the most wonderful squeaker."

I said I didn't like squeaky things unless they were mice.

"No," said the dog. "I suppose not."

And so we waited, for Warm and for Pest, and for the child. What a happy family we were.

Grace the Cat asks me, "Why is there no child here now? Did something come and eat him?"

"Eat him! No, he grew large and went to hunt in a new place. But he comes back to visit, and then we can jump on his bed and cry as if we were terribly hungry, and he will be fooled and come downstairs and feed us an early breakfast or a second supper. It is extremely handy to have him around."

"And will he pull my fur and bite my tail and fall down the steps?" Grace asks.

"He is just like the grown-ups now," I say with a sigh.

"Then why do we need him?" Grace the Cat asks me. "We have enough grown-ups."

"He is their kitten," I say.

"Oh," Grace says. "I see. Will we grow up and turn into grown-ups?"

"No, we are cats."

"And cats always stay cats?"

"Always."

Although, really, I am not so sure. I often dream that I am cleaning myself, and I notice that I have no fur, only skin like Warm's. I often dream that Warm picks me up and holds me against her, and she is covered with sweet-smelling fur, and her ears have grown tall and pointed, and when she nuzzles me with her nose, I feel her long whiskers twitch.

"And all children go away?" asks Grace, who is still thinking this over.

"Yes, they go away."

"But cats stay forever, and so they are more important and in every way more valuable," Grace says, and she begins to purr with contentment.

She is such a happy little cat. I do not think I will tell her all of my dog's story. What could she make of it?

"If only I could go out," Grace says. "Then I would be completely happy."

"It is not so wonderful out there. You can drown out there," I say.

"In the backyard?" Grace asks me.

"No, in the river near Mouse House."

"But we are not at Mouse House," says Grace. "Did you ever drown at Mouse House?"

"Do I look like I drowned?" I ask her.

But I almost did. Once I almost drowned in the river in front of Mouse House.

After the dog came back from the hospital, we resumed our trips to Mouse House. I was happy once more to find myself in the car with the dog. Still, I hid myself when I saw my blue box, but not very well. I made it easy for Warm to catch me. Under no circumstances did I want to be separated from my dog.

It was spring and the drive to Mouse House was as long as ever.

"I don't know if these trips in the car are good for the dog," said Pest, who had to lift the dog into the car because the dog could no longer climb in. But Warm said, "He loves that house so much that I think we should take him. He lies still in the car just the way he lies still on the floor. And he loves being out in the meadow."

"He runs around too much," Pest said.

"He lies down when his legs hurt him," Warm said.

"That's true," said Pest, and so we were off.

It had been some weeks since we had been to Mouse House, and during that time, I had begun hatching my plan. At Mouse House, I would pretend to be indifferent when Warm opened the door for the dog. And then, just when she no longer suspected trouble from me, I would dash through the door with the dog, and I would be out in the meadow at last. You won't be out long, I told my-

125

self, because the dog will get you by the collar and bring you back. But I was determined to get into the meadow, if only for a few minutes. If I was very lucky, I might hide beneath the bush Warm had planted when the child was born. The small bush was now the size of a tree, and very dense with twigs, and I thought, They will not be able to reach in to get me out and bring me back in. I will hide until dark and then walk around the house, and after that, I will come back and cry at the door. A cat should be allowed out once in his life!

My carefully hatched plans for escapes into the outside world never seemed to work, but this time I had planned properly.

In the morning, Warm went to the door to open it for the dog.

"Oh, look," she said. "The river is very high. I've never heard the river make so much noise."

There had been a great deal of snow, and when it melted, the river ran furiously. Warm went to the window to look at the river, which was usually invisible between its banks, but now it was as high as the riverbank and foamed as it made its way past the house.

"Stay away from the river," she said to the dog, and she patted his head and opened the door. She was not watching me at all and was taken by surprise when I suddenly dashed out behind the dog and ran as fast as I could across the meadow. I wanted to see the river, which the dog had told me was full of fish.

The dog saw me running through the grass and immediately began to run after me. He will get me and bring me back, I thought, and I have not even had a chance to find a mole hole on my own. I ran faster, and the dog, who was limping, had trouble keeping up with me. Still, I could hear him breathing behind me. I turned to look at him, and as I did, I lost my footing, skidded on some loose rocks at the top of the riverbank, and the next thing I knew I was tumbling downward, into the rushing water.

The dog ran along the bank shouting to me. "Keep your head up!" he shouted. "Cats can swim! Try to swim!"

But the water was so strong and fast I was helpless against it, and as I struggled to keep my head out of the water, I saw the river was about to take me under the bridge. I was passing a house I had never before seen—a blue house.

This is the end of all of my nine lives, I thought. I paddled with all my paws and I stretched my neck up high and I kept my nose out of the water, but finally I knew I was not strong enough to swim in a river as angry as this one. So this is how my mother felt when she went out to hunt and could not come back to me, I thought. And I closed my eyes, because I did not want to see any more of the terrifying river. I thought of the room in Mouse House, Warm and Pest sitting in their chairs, and I thought of my dog. I said goodbye to them all.

Suddenly I was grabbed by the neck, and still I did not open my eyes. I thought, A giant fish has me and he is about to eat me. But something was carrying me through the water, holding up my head so that water could not enter my nose or my mouth. When I opened my eyes, I saw that my dog had come for me. He had jumped into the river and grabbed me, and now he was swimming for the shore with all his strength.

We will both drown, I thought. But at least we will never be separated.

The dog, however, did not intend to drown. He swam through the black water with all his might, and I saw we were getting closer to the riverbank. I wanted to cry out *Keep going, keep going!* but I could not open my mouth because of the water that choked me, and because of the tight grip with which the dog held me in his mouth.

Really, I thought, my eyes filling with tears, he is a mighty animal. He is huge and strong and brave.

The water was cold. I was cold. I shivered, and I could feel the dog shiver beneath me. How long can he swim? I asked myself. I wonder when he will give up.

But he did not give up, and finally we came close to the riverbank, but it was slippery, and when the dog tried to climb out, he slid backward into the water. Then he tried again.

Pest was standing on the riverbank with a rope in his hands, and when the dog again tried to climb out of the river, he fastened the rope through the dog's collar, and began to pull him up. Finally, the two of us were on solid ground.

I waited for Pest to scold us, but he said nothing. Neither did Warm, who stood in back of him, crying. Pest picked me up and handed me to Warm, and then he patted the dog's head. "You take Foudini back in," he said. "I'll walk back slowly with Sam."

Warm began to carry me back to the house, but I twisted around in her arms to look at my dog. He was coming along in back of us, and he was limping badly.

Inside, Warm dried us both with towels. Then she took her hair dryer and dried the fur over the dog's back legs. After a while, she looked up at me and said, "Do you see what you've done? You almost drowned yourself and you almost drowned the dog. And now he is limping." She began to cry.

I climbed into her lap. I nuzzled her. I licked her face. But for the first time, she turned from me. She covered her face with her hands and continued to cry.

"Stop crying," said Pest. "The danger's over." This, of course, only made Warm cry harder.

"Both of them," said Warm, still crying. "Both of them at once!"

"They are *fine*," said Pest. "Just look at them!"

The dog was lying on his side, his mouth open, and I was lying across his teeth as I used to do.

"Don't you *ever* do that again!" said Warm, and I silently swore I would never do such a thing again.

"I am surprised we are both alive," I said to the dog later.

"So am I," he said. "It's been a long time since I swam the river retrieving sticks."

"But you knew you could save me," I said, nestling closer to him.

"I didn't know that," said the dog. "You would have done the same for me."

"I wouldn't have been of any use," I said. "I am an idiot, and I almost drowned you. I am a useless cat."

"You have done me more good than any other living thing," said the dog.

"Me?" I asked.

"You," said the dog.

"Me? Foudini?"

"You," Sam said.

"I have done *you* good?"

"Didn't I just say that?" Sam asked.

"But I am a useless cat!"

"Not if you can make someone love you," Sam said.

"Then you are not useless. You are *my* cat. My world was small and quiet before you came into it."

"I made it bigger?"

"Yes," Sam said. "You did."

I didn't know what to say, and so I didn't say anything. Instead, I burrowed into Sam's stomach until my head was hidden from view. Finally, I sat up and looked at Sam. "Do you mean to say you came for me because you love me? Is that what you mean?"

"I am your dog and you are my cat. That's why I jumped in after you. Of course I love you—even if you *are* a cat and I am a dog. Don't mention the river again."

I never did, and he never did.

And so I had my adventure in the meadow, and so I was nearly drowned, and worst of all, after that the dog's limp grew more pronounced than it had been before.

Was this a story to tell Grace the Cat? Perhaps when she is older and more sensible, I will tell her about the river and how strong the current was, and how cold the water was, and how dark, and how hard it was to breathe for days afterward because my lungs would not work properly. I will tell her how my dog had rescued me.

I was thinking this over—*my dog, my dog*—until it seemed to me I could hear his breathing, until it seemed to me I felt the warm air of his mouth as he licked my fur with his enormous tongue, and when I looked up, another cat, one I had never seen before, was standing over me.

"Don't get up," said this new cat. "It's easier for you to see me if you're sleeping. The stone cats sent me. I'm Snow White's cat. That part of my fur that is black is black as jet, and that part of my fur that is white is white as snow."

"Yes, you are a black-and-white cat," I said.

"And you are a black-and-white cat," she said. "But of course I am prettier. If you will tell me how pretty I am, I will tell you my secret name."

"You are a most pretty cat," I said. "Most splendid and most gorgeous." Any cat who lives with little Grace, and who wants his nose to stay unscratched, must grow experienced in giving compliments.

"My secret name is Ethel," Snow White's cat said.

"Ethel!"

"Oh, yes. We beautiful cats always take plain names. Our names remind us that there is more to life than beauty and that everyone is not as beautiful as we are. Although that little gray one sleeping there is beautiful." As she said this, she twitched her ears and her tail and narrowed her eyes, and my own tail began to twitch. I watched the new cat—Ethel!—carefully.

"I didn't come here to bother your cat. I came here to tell you a story. Probably you already know it.

"Once upon a time, there was a little girl whose hair

was black as coal, and whose skin was white as snow. Her mother did not like her, and so she found herself in the middle of a deep, dark wood where she fell asleep. A big cat found her there, and dragged her back to its den, where she grew up with the big cat's kittens and became good at climbing trees and speaking the language of cats. When the cats came back from hunting, she would comb out their fur with a comb she made out of twigs, and brush their fur with a brush she made of pine needles. Often, when they were away, she leaned against the tree outside their den and fell asleep, even though she had been told again and again that she must remain in the cave until her brothers and sisters came back.

"One day as she was sleeping, she felt something drop into her lap, and when she opened her eyes, she saw a bunch of beautiful purple grapes. Because it was a hot day and she was thirsty, she bit down on one of the grapes, and immediately she fell deeply asleep. When the cats came back from their hunt, they jumped about trying to wake her, but she slept on as if she were dreaming the most wonderful dream, and they thought, Oh, she will wake up later, and then she will brush us and comb us.

"But days passed and still she did not stir, and finally the smallest cat of all (that was me, you understand) climbed into her lap and began to cry. Of course, she thought that now the girl would wake up and begin to stroke her. But the girl continued to sleep, and in desperation the littlest cat pushed her head beneath the girl's hand, and then threw her little head back, so that the girl's hand moved against her. She was sure that the girl would wake up and remember to pet her as she always did. The girl, however, continued to sleep, and finally the little cat saw the purple grapes, which had begun to pucker and wither, and she did not like their smell.

"She sniffed the grapes and then she sniffed the girl's lips, and she understood that the girl had eaten the grapes. 'I am Snow White's cat,' she said, 'and if she eats these grapes, then I will eat them, too.' She ate one of the grapes, and she too fell asleep, right on the girl's lap.

"She slept and slept, next to Snow White, who was her Assigned Person, and she dreamed and dreamed, until even in her dreams she was sure she had used up all her nine lives, all her day lives *and* all her night lives. One day Snow White awakened. Her cat did, too. We were inside a glass box! And outside the box was a prince who let us out.

"When he let us out, he tried to chase me off. He said, 'Go away, you flea-bitten animal,' and he would have picked me up by the tail and thrown me deep into the forest. I was still weak, and he could easily have whirled me over his head, but the girl began to cry and said that she would not stay anywhere without her cat, and so the prince said that I could stay if she wanted me.

"So I lived with them for the rest of my life, and when I went to sleep one day and stopped moving, the prince was frightened out of his wits. He thought the girl would try to follow me right into the earth!

"He thought, I must find a way to keep the cat here with her, or she will go the way of that cat. He plucked hairs from my ears and my tail, and took them to a witch who baked them into a pie, and then they took the pie back to the girl and gave her the pie to eat, and as soon as she ate it, she began to mew and purr and flex her fingers as if she believed she had claws.

"That night when she fell asleep, there I was! I was lying around her neck, and my paws were on one of her shoulders, and my tail hung down from the other shoulder, and when she walked, she held on to my tail so I would not fall off, and we were just as we always were. She saw that we would never be separated, and we could never become separated, and she was happy to live on in the castle, because at night, when she slept, there I was.

"The prince did not know I was back, even though he could have seen me if he had looked into the girl's eyes, because I was there, in both her eyes, looking out at him. He never noticed me. And so we lived on together, even though, to his eyes, I was no longer there.

"Now, if you look in my eyes, you will see her in them. We are never separated from the ones we love. And if I look into your eyes, I will always see your dog in them. Although I must say," she said, yawning and beginning to waver, "that a dog is an exceedingly odd beloved to find in a good cat's eyes."

"Can you see him? He is really there?"

"He is really there. He is frighteningly large, and his tail is wagging."

"What color is he?" I asked. Ethel, Snow White's cat, might only be telling me what I hoped to hear.

"He is black and white and gray and brown and tan," she said. "And he has a red collar with diamonds on it."

"That is Sam," I said happily.

Grace the Cat is lying on her back, wriggling her way across the room, and while she wriggles, she cries. She says one word again and again, a word like "how," although she drags out the word so that it sounds like *ha-owww, ha-ooow,* and all the while, she keeps up the wormlike wriggling until she is right beneath my nose, and then she looks up at me, eagerly and expectantly.

When she gets up, she roams through the house screaming at the top of her lungs, making sounds I never imagined she could make. She no longer sounds like a cat, but an infant who is just learning to speak. It is even possible that she *will* be speaking within a few weeks. I have often heard Warm say that she thinks one day one of her cats will open its mouth and begin speaking, and that cat will be the Missing Link. Perhaps little Grace is the Missing Link. If she is, she is a very noisy, very wiggly Missing Link.

Grace is annoyed at me. She is shouting her head off. I think I will go down into the basement, climb into the rafters, and sleep in peace and quiet.

Ever since he had come back from the hospital, my dog limped. I had grown used to his limping, and how slowly he now walked, and how, after he rescued me from the river, he walked even more slowly, and now he often made little catlike cries when he first stood up. When we were fed, the dog would not get up immediately, and I often pushed the dish over to him with my head.

Whenever I could, I slept next to the dog and cleaned him, and on many days he would get up and chase me through the house, as he had done when I first came to live with him. But he was growing slower and slower, and although I told myself he was only lazy, I knew better.

Then one morning, he tried to get up, and his back legs once again would not obey him. Once again Warm and Pest carried him out to the car, and I knew they were taking him to the hospital. When I looked into his eyes, I knew that he did not expect to come back and that he had resigned himself to going to sleep in the wire cage and sleeping for a very long time, a longer time than either one of us could imagine. I saw all this in his eyes, although when Pest picked him up, he looked at me and said "Back soon," and for a moment, the dog wagged his tail briskly. But when Pest carried him out, I saw the dog did not turn around to look back at the house.

He *had* come back last time, and I believed he would come back again. This time I ate my dinner when it was served to me, and during the day, I slept on the couch and did not turn my back to the room. At night, I slept at the foot of the bed, because in that place the smell of my dog was so strong that I imagined he was still there.

During the day, I collected bits of the dog's fur on my tongue and hid them under the rug. I intended to mix them into my dish of steaming meat as soon as I had the chance. Nothing was ever going to separate *us*. I said to myself, I don't need a witch to bake his hairs into a pie. I am only doing what the witch would do if she were here. But, I thought, I must not let Warm see what I am doing. She will think I have gone mad and am deliberately eating up fur balls. I will wait until she puts out my food and goes upstairs, and then I will swallow the dog's fur, and we will never be parted. He will come to me at night as long as I live.

Every day Warm and Pest would get in the car and come back smelling of the hospital and the dog, but the dog did not come back with them. Then one day, Warm came back, crying, and Pest sat next to her on the couch and didn't say anything, and he picked me up and set me down in his lap, which ordinarily he never did, and I understood that the dog would not be coming back.

Warm cried and said my dog was such a good dog. He hardly ever barked. He thought everyone coming to the door wanted to see him. He was not at all suspicious natured, as I was.

"He wouldn't have barked unless someone had tried to break into the house dressed in a cat suit. He barked at other cats, remember? Probably he thought they'd hurt Foudini," Pest said. "I never understood what he saw in that animal."

At this, Warm cried even harder, and I, who cannot cry easily, twitched my tail in sheer misery.

I tried to follow Warm through the house so that she could pet me while she cried. I thought that perhaps if I was a good cat, my dog would somehow come back, but when he did not come back even though I was a good cat and patiently waited, I did again turn my back to the room. To make matters worse, it seemed to me that it was growing warmer in the house, and whenever Warm or Pest came downstairs, I looked over my shoulder to see if they had brought the large gray boxes down with them.

"That cat is going to die himself if we don't do something," Warm said.

Pest said he didn't want any more pets.

"Not a pet for *us*," Warm said. "A pet for the *cat*."

" 'A pet for the cat'—don't be ridiculous," Pest said.

"We *are* going to get another cat," Warm said, and Pest said I didn't even know I was a cat. I growled instead of purred, and I lay on the sofa as if I were a dog, sprawled in every direction, and I chewed happily on dog biscuits. What made her think I would accept another cat? What made her think I wouldn't attack a kitten and try to kill it? What made her think I would put up with another cat sitting on her lap, when it was plain to see that I thought *I* was her owner?

"He is a good and loving cat, and he will love whatever cat we get to keep him company, especially if it's a kitten," Warm said.

"And if he doesn't?" Pest asked.

"He will," said Warm.

"That's why they came to look for me?" asked little Grace. "Because *you* refused to get up and chase mice through the house? They got *me* to cheer *you* up?"

"Of course they looked at many cats before they decided on you," I said, which was not true at all. Warm told the lady who grooms her hair that she wanted another cat, and the lady said she just happened to have one. Warm should come by and see if she liked it, and Pest said, "You know if you look at the cat, you will decide that's the cat you want," which, of course, happened. This explanation, however, would not suit little Grace at all.

"How did they decide on me?" asked Grace. "Was it my beautiful tail, or the lovely tufts of fur in my ears?"

"I think they particularly liked the tufts of fur between the pads of your paws," I said. "Those tufts of fur you never quite lick clean."

"Oh," said little Grace, holding up a paw and examining it, "what lovely paws they are, too. How did it escape my notice?"

"So you see you come from the country near Mouse House, and when you settle down a bit, you should be an excellent mouser."

"I *am* an excellent mouser," said the exasperating little Grace, who cannot sit still even for a minute, and who even now is beginning to wiggle across the room on her way to the heating vent through which warm air is blowing.

"I hope you are not starting that noise again," I said. "How terrible you sound, worse than a human baby!"

"I have to make noise, when you don't understand anything!" said Grace the Cat.

"I am older than you are, and I understand whatever you understand and more," I said, and Grace the Cat looked sullen and said, "Not everything."

Just then, Warm and Pest came into the room, whispered together, and stared at me.

"*Packing alert, packing alert,*" I said to Grace, who only yawned and said she didn't know about me, but she didn't mind riding in a car, if, when she got out again, she found herself in Mouse House climbing on the pile of logs Warm and Pest brought in from the woodshed, logs full of wonderful smells and even, occasionally, a small black bug that crunched when you chewed it.

"But," said Grace, "I don't see any packing boxes. I don't see any trash bags with books and sweaters stuffed into them. In my opinion, they are not going."

"They are up to something," I said.

They were, but it was not packing.

The next day, three men came to the house and went down into the basement, my safest place. They began walking around the furnace, looking at it, and banging on it, and even grabbing hold of one of its metal arms and wrenching it off!

"How old is this thing?" asked one of the men.

"It's an antique," said another man.

"It's got to go," said the first man.

They fell upon my faithful furnace and tore it to pieces.

I ran upstairs, wailing loudly. Warm ought to rush down and stop them! Where would I sleep? Wasn't it already growing cold now that the furnace had stopped its noisy breathing and rattling?

"Don't worry," said Warm. "It will be warm again tomorrow."

When it was quiet once more, I went downstairs to inspect the furnace. It had been lifted from the floor. Most of its arms had been torn off and strewn about. The men were sitting on the steps, eating their sandwiches.

I snuck up onto the furnace's one remaining arm, and from there climbed onto a rafter that led beneath the living room floor, and I went along it as far in as I possibly could. I had never been in here before—between the basement ceiling and the living room floor—it was dusty. At first I sneezed, but I soon fell asleep.

I was awakened by the most terrifying noise, the sound of the furnace screaming at me as the men did something to its metal skin. The stone cats say that one day the world will come to an end, and you will know when that happens because everything that has stayed the same will change. There will be fearsome noises, and fires will break out everywhere. The furnace had never before said a word, and now it was screaming and screaming. I have grown to be a secure and happy cat, but I am not so foolish as to forget what an unsafe place the world can be. I crept farther beneath the living room floor until I was tightly sandwiched between the underside of that floor and the ceiling of the basement play-room. The world went on ending for hours and hours. The furnace screamed constantly. There was a great hammering and banging that shook the walls of the house, and finally it was quiet. Even though it was quiet, I could not stop shaking.

Warm came down into the basement and began calling me. *Foudini! Foudini!* She called me again and again. She mewed for me in her best cat voice. But I would not come out. The world had come to an end, and now there was only dust and ash and terrible men who made the furnace scream.

Warm took a broom and began poking it into my cus-tomary hiding places, but she did not find me. Soon Pest came down, and he climbed up to the rafters and began shining a light into the darkest places, looking for me. But I was at the end of a long and narrow tunnel, and I am a black cat, except for my white lightning streak, and I turned my head away and covered my nose with my paws. He could not see me.

After a while, they left. I will never come down, I thought.

I heard Warm, outside, calling *Foudini! Foudini!* I was not coming out, even though I was hungry and knew I would be growing hungrier still. I thought about Grace the Cat, and hoped she had been in a good place when the world came to an end.

"The world has not come to an end," said an enormous golden cat. "The world comes to an end only once, and usually when it does, we do not even know it."

I picked up my head and sniffed. The golden cat had no smell, and so I knew he was a dream cat.

"They have destroyed the furnace I loved so much, and now I have nowhere to sleep and nothing to climb back down on," I said. "Don't tell me the world hasn't come to an end."

"There is a ladder right there," said the golden cat. "You can climb down that ladder whenever you want to. There is a plate of food on the floor, so you need not be hungry. Believe me, the world has not come to an end, not for you. There is still Grace the Cat, who is upstairs crying for you even as she sleeps. You might think about leaving this hiding place, good hiding place as it is."

The golden cat had crawled into my tunnel with me, and I thought that if he could find his way to me, so might Warm.

"Oh, I don't know about that," said the golden cat. "I am good at tunneling through dark and narrow and mysterious places. After all, I have had a lifetime of practice."

I asked him whose cat he was.

"I am Freud's cat," he said. "He would take a dim view of your behavior today, I must tell you, your little wife up there crying and wiggling, while you hide yourself between the ceiling and the floor because a loud noise has scared you."

"Who is this Assigned Person Freud?" I asked him, and he said Freud was a strange man who spent most of his time in a room listening to people who lay on couches, and sometimes these people came to lie on his couch for years, and afterward they felt much better and went on to live happy lives filled with kittens and cats.

"I lie on a couch all the time," I said, "and when I get up and jump down, I am no happier than I was before, only less tired or more bored."

"It must have had something to do with the stories they told him," said Freud's cat, "although you have never heard such stories! Tales of how mothers pinched their cheeks! Tales of how hot the porridge was and how it burned their throats! Someone kissing the cook in the kitchen, probably because she had baked a very good mouse pie. Ridiculous stories about sheep climbing into trees at night and staring at you in your bedroom. When everyone knows sheep can't climb trees! *We* can climb trees! Not sheep! I don't know how many times I had to hear this preposterous story about sheep in the trees. And did Freud ever say, *Sheep cannot climb trees*? No, he did not. Not very exciting stories, if you ask me," he said, and began to lick his front paw.

"But of course when they lay on the couch, I was not permitted to lie there, and I did resent that, you know, although when I spoke to Freud about it, he said, 'We must all resign ourselves to the inevitable.' What did the inevitable have to do with people taking my place on the couch? I *could* have slept on the armrest above their heads! There was plenty of room for me. I could have kept quiet. They wouldn't even have known I was there!

"But he said they would know I was there, and I had to understand—a cat is not always a cat. And I said, 'No, that isn't true. A cat *is* always a cat.' That was why we didn't come trooping into his office and lie upon his couch and talk to him one hour a day, day after day, for years.

"I believe he learned quite a lot from me," said the golden cat. "His desk was cluttered with little statues and bits of stone, and he would watch me as I walked across his desk, or along his shelves, never disturbing anything or knocking anything over, and one day he said, 'Yes, that is the way we must walk in our practice, carefully and not disturbing the dust until it is ready to be disturbed.' Of course I had no idea what he meant. I rarely understood what he meant. Unless, of course, he was ordering me down from the couch.

"But how unreasonable he was! There were dozens of pillows on that couch, and how many heads does a human have? One of those pillows ought to have been mine! All he had to do was say, 'See here! You have more

pillows than anyone needs! One of them is for my cat!'
That would have been the end of it. But instead he said,
'While they are here, that couch is their kingdom.' A
couch a kingdom! Well, if that was their kingdom, then
they were welcome to it! But when he left the room, of
course I made mincemeat of his rubber plant!

"When he saw that, how he scolded me. I wanted to
know how he knew I was the guilty party. And he said,
'Who else would chew the leaves and leave such teeth
marks?' And when I looked at the leaves, I could plainly
see that only a cat could have chewed them up. And so
the next time I attacked the plant, I left the leaves alone
and dug the stem out from beneath the dirt and chewed
through its bark, and I was happy to see the rubber plant
begin to wilt and sag. Finally it shriveled up and turned
brown altogether.

"But Freud promptly replaced it with another, healthy
rubber plant. 'Leave this one alone,' he told me, and I
said I had nothing to do with the other one and its rubber blight problems, and he said, 'Rubber blight! It was
you at the leaves!' I said I hadn't touched the leaves, not
once, after he scolded me.

" 'Then it is a great mystery,' he said, 'and I will get to
the root of it.'

"But he never did. Many rubber plants came and went
and still, *still,* I did not get my place on a pillow. And at
night, I came in and sharpened my claws on the rugs he

spread over his couch, but he put an end to that soon enough. 'I will have your claws taken out,' he said. I said that was unfair. People came in and told him stories about how they scratched out their little brother's or sister's eyes, and he never threatened to pull out *their* nails.

" 'Well, it is a very different matter,' he said. 'After all, they are human beings. But you! If you do not start to behave, I will cut off your tail!'

"Naturally, that frightened me, and I resolved to be good, but even so, as I lay under the couch on the hard floor, and heard the patient's voice coming to me through the leather and the springs and the horsehair, I would grow more and more furious. There were times when a patient let his hand hang down, and I could not resist. I would swat at the hand moving back and forth. When I did, I could feel Freud's burning eyes upon me, although there were times when he did not look at all angry. There were times when he smiled at me happily, as if he wished I would swat at that hand again, this time with my claws out.

"He never did remove my claws, and of course, as you can see, I still have my tail," said the golden cat. "But you, if you are going to lie above this ceiling like a dead cat on a couch, I have something to tell you. Grace the Cat is not such a little cat any longer. She wriggles beneath your nose, and she cries to you, and you ignore her. Surely you know what she wants."

"She wants to make a nuisance of herself," I said. "It is what she always wants."

"She wants kittens," said Freud's cat.

"Kittens? Kittens? Kittens come to houses in boxes, as I came to this house."

"Think back," said the golden cat. "Were you always a kitten in this house?"

"No, once I was a kitten who lived in a basement."

"And before that?"

"Before that I was a kitten who lived in a wall."

"And before that?"

"Before that," I said, thinking back—but I could not think of anything before the wall.

"Think harder," said Freud's cat.

And suddenly I was in a warm, dark place, and there was a wonderful sound, *thud, thud, thud,* deep and regular, and the sound of someone breathing in and out, and when whoever that was breathed in, something pressed me gently and then let me go, as if I were being petted, and there was the sound of water that also pressed against me and let me go, and a low, growling sound, and as soon as I heard that, I knew I was again hearing the voice of my mother.

But where was she?

And then I understood that she was all around me.

"Before the wall, I was in my mother's belly," I said. "I think that's where I was."

"You were there," Freud's cat said. "You see how superior we are to human beings? In only a few minutes, you have hunted down the very beginnings of your life. Now you will be a most happy cat." He said this with complete confidence.

"Why will I be a happy cat?" I asked him. "All I have done is remember more about the mother I lost. Now I will miss her all over again."

"Stupid!" he said. "Must I tell you everything? Your mother was a *female* cat. Grace the Cat is a *female* cat. Now do you see?"

I did see. I was shocked.

I asked him if he meant to say that my mother had wiggled and shrieked her way across floors, because certainly she had not. Surely she had been a proper cat, a perfect cat, the model of propriety. *She* had not climbed to the roofs of garages and howled her head off, as outside cats did here.

"I think she may have wiggled," Freud's cat said mildly.

"Not my mother," I said.

"Then what are you doing here?" Freud's cat asked me. "If she did not wiggle? If a certain black cat didn't see her wiggle and climb up on her and bite her on the shoulder."

"Climb up on her and bite her on the shoulder?" In spite of myself, I was curious.

"Sometimes, he bit her on her hind leg," he said. "That, too."

"Grace the Cat would not like that," I said confidently. "Grace the Cat does not like to be bitten, or to have me lie down on top of her because I am so heavy. Grace the Cat likes to bite *me,* and she does, *all* the time."

"When they wiggle, they are not the same as they are otherwise," he said. How positive this cat always sounded!

"It makes no difference to me," I said. "I am not coming down. It is the end of the world, and besides that, I am afraid of ladders."

"But if you listen, if you press your ear against the underside of the living room floor, you can hear Grace crying for you. You can hear every word she's saying."

I did press my ear to the underside of the living room floor. "She is saying she wishes I would come back and sing her her good-night song," I said.

"If the world had ended, would she want you to come and sing to her?"

"She might. She is a very spoiled cat," I said.

"Sing your song to Grace the Cat, and perhaps she will hear you through the floorboards."

"We do not need songs at the end of the world," I said, but I began to sing nevertheless, the night song I always sang to Grace, the song I had sung before to my dog, who liked it enormously, and who, when I sang, would growl his strange growl that was so much like a purr.

> *People live in houses*
> *All filled with mouses*
> *And that is why they need a cat like me*
> *Who catches all the mice for free.*
>
> *Open up the back porch door,*
> *Leave some crumbs upon the floor,*
> *All I need is food to eat,*
> *And mouses, mouses, mouses!*
>
> *Once there was a neighborhood*
> *With three ravens in a wood*
> *But there were no mouses there*
> *Running under easy chairs,*
>
> *So I said, It's time to go,*
> *I must hunt my mice, you know,*
> *All I need is food to eat,*
> *And mouses, mouses, mouses!*
>
> *Open up the back porch door,*
> *Leave some crumbs upon the floor,*
> *All I need are sunny days,*
> *And mouses, mouses, mouses!*

"That last part is a refrain," I said, trying to look as modest as possible. "Sometimes it is 'food to eat' and sometimes it is 'sunny days,' and sometimes it is other things, depending on what enters my mind. That is my own song."

"Freud always said art was the highest of human pursuits," he said.

"And would he have liked my song?" I asked him, and he said he was sure Freud would have liked my song, although he would have asked me many questions about the three ravens in a wood. I said the ravens were in a wood because, as everyone knew, poems had to rhyme, and "wood" rhymed with "neighborhood," so the question-and-answer session would not take very long.

"He would ask you why you thought of the word 'neighborhood,' " said Freud's cat. "You might have thought of another word altogether. You might, for example, have said 'couches' instead of 'easy chairs.' "

"And I might not have thought up the song at all!" I cried.

Freud's cat sighed and watched me through narrowed eyes. "My person could not have had a very easy life," he said. "Will you sing that song to Grace the Cat?"

"If you think it is a very good song."

"It is a very good song. In my opinion."

So I sang my song to Grace at the top of my lungs.

When I stopped, I could hear her listening. I could hear her breathing, right through the floorboards.

"What are you going to do tomorrow?" Freud's cat asked me, and I said I would find a way to come down from these rafters. Then I would jump upon Grace the Cat, and bite her on the neck, and see what happened next.

Freud's cat seemed quite pleased, and began to waver and tremble as these ghost cats always do when they are about to take their leave. "You can call me anytime, day or night."

By now, he was a mere outline shimmering in the darkness. Then he was gone.

I was alone again, and I was sleepy, so I put my head down on my paw. I must have fallen asleep, because a rough paw on my shoulder suddenly shook me awake.

"I see you are up to your old tricks," said my dog. "Nothing ever changes."

"Is that you?" I asked, my heart filling with happiness. But then I grew angry. Why had he hidden himself away for so long? "Where have you been hiding?" I asked him.

"On the other side of the door," said the dog. "You were right, you know. There is a door we can open to go from the city house to Mouse House."

"I told you so," I said.

"But I had to go a long way to find it," said my dog.

"That is because you are so stubborn. If you had looked for it when I told you to look for it, we would have been saved all those rides in the car."

"I couldn't have found it then," said my dog. "Come down from the ceiling, and I'll show it to you."

"I'm not coming down," I said. And I asked him if he had just come back from the hospital.

"Open your eyes," my dog said.

I opened them, and when I did, I saw my dog shimmered and quivered just as the ghost cat had done. My dog! He was back!

"Yes, I am back," said my dog. "You mixed my fur into your food and ate it, so I was able to come back to you."

"After I mixed your fur in my food, I had a stomach ache," I said. "Night after night, I looked for you, but you didn't come."

"It took me longer than I thought to make up a new Map of Smells," my dog said. "After all, I live somewhere else now. I would start out to see you and get lost. But I heard everyone calling out for you, and I thought I had better hurry. Your poor person! She believes you escaped through the basement door the workmen left open. She has been walking through the neighborhood with a spoon and a tin of canned mice, calling your name, and as she walks, she taps on the tin. She stops and looks under bushes, and she climbs onto people's porches and looks for you under their chairs. Soon everyone will think she is mad. Is this a way for a cat to behave to his Assigned Person?"

"I have not been very good," I said grudgingly.

"You have been terrible," said the dog.

"I have been terrible," I agreed happily.

"You admit it?" my dog asked, astonished.

"I would admit to anything," I said. "I am so happy to see you."

"Let's go out in the meadow," said my dog. "There are plenty of moles and a family of chipmunks. I'll carry you by your neck just as your mother used to."

"We can't go out in the meadow," I said. "We are back in the city house. You came a long way and you are confused."

He picked me up and jumped down from the ceiling with me in his mouth and crossed the basement to a dark corner.

"The door is right here," he said, "behind this screen."

The door was there. It opened for us, and we were out in the meadow.

"Oh, moles, moles, moles!" I cried out with delight, and I began digging happily down into a hole in the grass.

"Without looking to the right or left," my dog said with a sigh. "You must be careful, even though I am with you."

I stopped digging and looked around me.

"It is quite safe," I said. "No one else is here."

"You should find that out first," said my dog. "Not after you have begun merrily digging. A bear's mouth is not as nice a mouth to be in as mine is."

"Let's run across the meadow," I said. "Can you run?"

"I can run as fast as I ever could," said my dog. "Let's run to the river. It's quiet these days. Only don't go too close to the rim. There are many pebbles and loose stones, and your foot will slide, and you will be back in the water."

We ran across the meadow, and I leaped into the air and caught orange-and-black butterflies and white moths and even a baby swallow that had swooped down too low, but as soon as I felt my dog's eyes on me, I released the small bird, and it flew swiftly away.

"The smells, the smells!" I said. "Such wonderful smells!" I bit off pieces of grass. I chewed on a dry leaf. I pressed my nose up against a tree. I leaped into the air after a firefly.

"I am so glad I had you to come back to," said my dog. "If you hadn't summoned me, I would never have smelled the smells of this meadow again."

"You would have!" I said.

"No," said my dog. He said, "Let's run across the meadow again."

And so we ran and ran, and I leaped after frogs and

salamanders and large beetles, and I batted at flowers waving in the breeze, until finally my dog and I were tired, and we lay down in the sun. I lay on one of the dog's front paws and licked his nose with my rough tongue.

"I never thought I would like to feel that tongue on my nose," said my dog. "But now it is the most wonderful feeling."

We lay there until the light began to fade.

"I think we should go back," the dog said. "Everyone is looking for you."

"Will you come back again?" I asked him. "Promise you will come back!"

"You won't see me, but I will be there, and you will know I am there because you will feel my breath on your fur."

"Can I tell Grace the Cat about you?" I asked, and my dog said that Grace was still a very young cat. Perhaps I should let her learn about ghost cats and dogs when she was ready.

"Perhaps she is ready now," I said, "wiggling and crying as she does. She sings such mad songs. I wish you could hear them."

"I have," said my dog. "Horrible!"

"But she is not so bad," I said.

"No," said my dog.

"I love her," I said. I looked guiltily at the dog.

"You are *my* dog," I said. "You are my one and only dog!"

"That is enough for me," he said. We were back in the basement in my hiding place beneath the living room floor, and he began to waver, and finally he disappeared. But I could smell the odor of his fur all around me. He really had come back to me!

The next day, Warm came down to the basement and began to call me again. *Foudini! Foudini! Foudini!*

Her voice was so piteous that I began to feel sorry for her. I crept forward in my dark tunnel until my head was sticking out and she could see me, and when she did, what a shriek of joy flew from her mouth!

"He is down here! He's down here! He's here!" she shouted again and again until Pest himself came running, and right behind him was little Grace, who began mewing ecstatically.

"How will we get him down from there?" asked Warm, and Pest said, "I will put a board up against the ceiling, and he can walk down when he's ready."

Walk all the way down from the ceiling on a board? Walk from the ceiling to the floor on a narrow plank? A cat of my size?

"If we pushed that chest of drawers beneath him," Warm said, "he could jump down onto it. It's not far."

"Put his dish on the chest," said Pest. "Food is all he's interested in."

For that, I thought, I will stay up here until evening.

Which is what I did. And when I came down, I was hugged almost to death by Warm and carried off with her to bed, and when Pest said I was on *his* pillow and *his* side of the bed, Warm said I could have her side of the bed, and she would balance herself on the bed's edge, and so I moved toward her. I did not want her falling out of the bed and hobbling about on sticks, as she had once done when the child was still small.

It was not until the next day that I climbed up on little Grace (who was not, just as Freud's cat had said, so little as I thought), and I bit her on the neck, and to my astonishment, she was very happy to be bitten, and followed me about all day, licking and grooming me.

This is not bad, I thought. I think I like this, I thought. What a lovely cat she is. Why did I never realize it before?

"You have such beautiful gray fur," I told Grace. "And such beautiful round yellow eyes."

"I know," said Grace.

"You are really *very* beautiful," I said.

"Yes, I am," said Grace.

"I suppose I am lucky to have you," I said.

"Yes, you are," said Grace. "I am your cat."

She was. She was my cat.

And it was not until I was once more back in bed with Warm and Pest and little Grace that I realized the world had not come to an end.

Time passed, as it must. Many nights, I went down to the foot of the bed, because I smelled the dog's fur and knew he was there.

A new furnace, square and shiny and ugly, came to take the place of the old one with its many arms. The round hole in the basement floor, left behind when the old furnace was destroyed, was cemented up, and a rug was placed on the floor where the old furnace had once been. A green fainting couch was put there also, and we found this couch very convenient, because it was always warm in the basement in the winter, and cool in the summer, and so we would lie upon it.

Then one day, Grace vanished, and we began searching for her, but we could not find her.

"She is here somewhere," said Warm. "She could not get out."

"Unless she found a way through the rafters to the outside," said Pest, who is a terrible pessimist and will think of something to worry us if he can.

"Find her, find Grace," Warm told me, but her smell was everywhere, and I could not find her.

The next day, Warm and I were sitting on the living

room couch when out of thin air Grace appeared. She sat on the rug in front of us and looked up at us.

"What is that she has in her mouth?" Warm asked. "Has she got a mouse? Or is it a sock? It looks like a wet sock."

I looked at Grace's mouth. Whatever she had between her teeth, it wasn't a mouse. There was no mouse smell at all.

"I think it is a sock," Warm said, and just then, Grace lay the gray thing down on the rug in front of us, and it stirred and made a small meeping sound.

"It's a kitten!" Warm said, and she started to get up to look more closely at it, but Grace twitched her tail and lowered her head as if to grab the kitten back up between her teeth. Then she looked at us as if she expected something to happen.

"Oh, it is a beautiful, beautiful kitten!" said Warm. "What a beautiful, beautiful kitten you have!"

This must have been what Grace was waiting for, because her face grew all blurry and happy, and she picked up the little wet gray thing and carried it out of the room.

"She wanted to show it to us!" said Warm. "A kitten! And they said you wouldn't know what to do if you'd been raised alone without other cats!"

Wrong again, I thought.

"Of course, we'll have to give some of them away," Warm said.

Some of them!

"Because usually there are five or six."

Five or six!

There were five, although one of them never began to move, and when I discovered Grace's hiding place, she told me to go away because she would have to eat that one, and I don't know if she did, but when I came back the little one who would not move was gone.

And in no time at all, the four kittens were leaping about beneath the couch in the basement, and in no time at all, they were all sneezing, and their eyes were sticky and crusty, as mine had once been.

Pest and Warm packed them up and took them to the hospital, where they were pricked with sharp needles and then sent home again, the hospital smell on them.

And they began to grow, and two of them were packed into boxes and went off with people who came to look at them. This made Grace the Cat unhappy, but Warm told her again and again that they were going home with people who would take care of them as she herself had been taken care of. Grace was so busy with the two remaining kittens, who still pushed themselves beneath her stomach trying to drink from her stomach faucets, and the kittens chased her and pounced on her from morning until night.

And we are all happy now. Warm and Pest are happy. I am happy with Grace and the two kittens, who any day now will discover mirrors and who will soon enough begin listening to the stories we intend to tell them about our lives as housecats.

I have not yet told Grace about the ghost cats who come to visit me in dreams.

Grace is still too young to understand any of this—at least, that is my opinion—and she will not understand until she grows older and the ghost cats come to visit her. I do not think my dog will come to visit her.

Every night, I sing my song to the kittens, who now spend the nights with Grace in the basement. And after all, the shiny new furnace is warmer than the old one, and there is little for us to complain of.

"They can sleep with us when they stop leaping about all night," says Pest.

I wish the dog would come back again. Sometimes I wish we had another dog, but of course we cannot have everything. There are times I think the dog does come at night when I sleep, and in the morning, sometimes the faint smell of his fur lingers in the air.

Soon the four of us will sleep with Warm and Pest in the warm bed whose windows are tickled by branches of the squirrelly tree outside. Snow will soon begin flying against the windows once more, and the squirrels will leave black paw prints as they jump from branch to branch, and so we will all settle down for a long winter's sleep.

I have done as I promised and told you the story of my life, the story that is still going on, Foudini M. Cat (*M* is for "Mouser"), housecat of city house and Mouse House, my story written by myself, every word of it true.

© Jerry Bauer

ABOUT THE AUTHOR

Susan Fromberg Schaeffer was born in Brooklyn and
educated at the University of Chicago,
where she received her Ph.D. in 1966. She is the author
of ten other novels and five books of poetry.
She lives in New York.